# BORN IN BROOKLYN
## JOHN MONTAGUE'S AMERICA

## John Montague

### Edited by David Lampe

WHITE PINE PRESS

© 1991 John Montague

All rights reserved. This book, or parts thereof, may not be reproduced in any form without permission.

The publication of this book was made possible, in part, by grants from the National Endowment for the Arts and the New York State Council on the Arts.

Some of the poems, stories and essays have appeared in: *Figures In A Cave, Death of a Chieftain, The Dead Kingdom, A Slow Dance, A Chosen Light, Poison Lands, The Rough Field, Forms of Exile, Tides, The Great Cloak,* and *Mount Eagle.*

Design by Watershed Design

Cover photograph: Keith Gemerek

Photograph of John Montague by John Reeves

Printed in the United States of America

ISBN 1-877727-13-x

WHITE PINE PRESS
76 Center Street
Fredonia, N.Y. 14063

Photograph: Keith Gemerek

*For Bill, Tom, and The Writers Institute*

## CONTENTS

Introduction / 1
from The Figure in the Cave / 9
A Muddy Cup / 16
Mother Cat / 19
A Flowering Absence / 21
The Locket / 24
The Letters / 26
The Complex Fate of Being American-Irish / 32
The Country Fiddler / 37
Stele for a Northern Republican / 38
The Fault / 40
The Cage / 41
A Christmas Card / 43
The Oklahoma Kid / 45
Respect / 59
A Graveyard in Queens / 61
Downtown, America / 65
Visible Export / 65
Cultural Center / 66
American Landscapes:
    I—Ghost Town / 68
    II—Bus Stop in Nevada / 68
    III—Hollywood and Vine / 68
Earthbound
    I—Newsreel / 69
    II—Field Theory / 70
    III—Earthbound / 71
Do Not Disturb / 72
Gone / 73
Talisman / 74
All Legendary Obstacles / 75
William Carlos Williams, 1955 / 76
Death of a Chieftain / 77
Coatlicue / 102
Company / 103
Beyond the Liss / 104

A Ballad for Berryman / 106
Sinnsear: Kindred / 107
Vietnam / 108
Bluegrass / 109
Pacific Legend / 110
A Slow Dance / 111
The Evolving Logos / 112
Poetry Class / 113
Magic Carpet / 114

# BORN IN BROOKLYN

*What am I doing here?*
*(After all, I was born in the damn place!)*

**THE CITY OF NEW YORK,**
**DEPARTMENT OF HEALTH.**

**STATE OF NEW YORK**

Registered Number **9595**

## CERTIFICATE AND RECORD OF BIRTH
### OF

| | | | | | |
|---|---|---|---|---|---|
| Name of Child | John Patrick Montague | | | | |
| Sex | M. | Color or Race | W. | Mother's Marriage Name | Mary Montague |
| Date of Birth | Feb. 28, 1929 | | | Mother's Name Before Marriage | Mary Carney |
| Place of Birth Street, No. and Borough | St. Catherine's Hospital | | | Mother's Residence | Same |
| Father's Name | James Montague | | | Mother's Birthplace | Ireland |
| Father's Residence | 56 Rodney St. | | | Mother's Age | 31 | Color | W. |
| Father's Birthplace | Ireland | | | Mother's Occupation | Hwf. |
| Father's Age | 39 | Color | W | Number of Children Born to this Mother including Present Birth | 3 |
| Father's Occupation | Grocery Clerk | | | Number of Children of this Mother Now Living | 3 |

I, the undersigned, hereby certify that I attended professionally at the above birth and I am personally cognizant thereof; and that all the facts stated in said certificate and report of birth are true to the best of my knowledge, information and belief.

Signature _A. P. Mac Veay_ PHYSICIAN / MIDWIFE

DATE OF REPORT, ................19... Residence ................

# *Introduction*

> —all mythologies are local,
> courage related to time and place.

Born in Brooklyn in 1929 after his father had left Ireland during "the troubles," John Montague's mother would remember his delivery at St. Catherine's Hospital, Bushwick Avenue, as "the worst birth in the annals of Brooklyn." Montague then lived in Brooklyn with his two older brothers for the first four years of his life until, as he conjectures, the end of prohibition and the death of his uncle John, who "ran a wild speakeasy, and died of it," forced their return to Ulster, where the family was "shared out" and he was "fostered" by his father's sisters, seven miles away from his mother and brothers in Fintona. This separation is powerfully and poignantly recalled in *Dead Kingdom,* which evokes scenes of lost family harmony and the pain of separation. A number of earlier poems also attempt to recreate this shattered world of family closeness and the now lost world of Irish Brooklyn "among gasoline fumes, run-down brownstones." This was the "muddy cup" his mother "refused to drink." That Brooklyn slum where he was born, the present Williamsburg, was, she was certain, "not respectable."

> (cops and robbers,
> cigarstore Indians
> & coal black niggers,

bathtub gin and
Jewish neighbors)
—"A Muddy Cup"

The crash of 1929, just months after a painful breech birth, convinced her of the emptiness of the tawdry "American Dream." When she contracted tuberculosis, she made arrangements to send her sons back to safer, saner Northern Ireland.

Though that wooden Indian was gone when he returned fifty-two years later to another "wild, raunchier Brooklyn," the old moviehouse was still there "with its matinee of monsters and Mickey Mouse," as was the library he had visited with his older brother Seamus and, finally, the old elevated railroad. "When I climbed the steps to the platform of the old El," he explains, "I instinctively reached for a larger, taller hand." That presence was his father, "the least happy / man I have known," who worked behind the "grille / in the Clark Street I.R.T." and who taught his young son "to croon Ragtime Cowboy / Joe swaying in his saddle / as he sings." This awareness of past and present, of pain and pleasure, certainly explains the doubleness of experience and vision in "The Oklahoma Kid." This story comically juxtaposes the local Irish country perspective with distant "prairies of imagination," the prosaic fact with romantic fiction. An imaginative ten-year-old boy raised by two maiden aunts finds himself in a world "speculative only about local things" epitomized by Peter Anthony Cummins (Papa), a non-stop talker who has never seen a movie and who "stuck straight through it to whatever everyday life he could recognize." This disastrous experience is harrowing for the young narrator, who admits "not only could I scarcely remember my life in America, but I could hardly remember even my father." Yet it ends with a coda of American affirmation and experience seventeen years later:

> Eating a sour mess of beef and hash, I began a conversation with the man beside me. He seemed somehow familiar—that great nose, that coppery tint (noticeable even under a day-old beard), those wise eyes of legend.
>
> "I'm a Cherokee from Tulsa," he said, with what I took to be both fatalism and pride. "What part of Oklahoma do you come from?"
>
> "From Oklahoma City," I said involuntarily, "County

Tyrone," and choked with a mixture of joy, shame, and ridiculous conceit.

"Death of a Chieftain," the title story of Montague's collection of short stories, reverses this process in a story that seems to have anticipated "magic realism" and that has its wandering Irishman, Bernard Corruna Coote, find tribal and mythic fulfillment in an ancient rite performed in a passage grave in Central America. The popular music group The Chieftains take their name from this story. Montague's most recent story, "The Letters," appearing in print for the first time here, draws on a cache of family letters to explore how the immediate harshness of the Brooklyn environment was made worse by increasing economic problems and the shattering effect reading them has on the "runt of the litter."

Unlike his mother, who would find security in her return to Fintona, the imprint of America would remain present in both thought and language for young Montague. In an Irish schoolroom he was "taunted" by a teacher who, he explains, "had hunted" him "down / to near speechlessness."

*So this is our brightest infant?*
*Where did he get that outlandish accent?*
*What do you expect, with no parents,*
*sent back from some American slum:*
*none of you are to speak like him!*

Stammer, impediment, stutter:
she had found my lode of shame,
and soon I could no longer utter
those magical words I had begun
to love, to dolphin delight in.

And not for two stumbling decades
would I manage to speak straight again.
Grounded for the second time
my tongue became a rusted hinge
until the sweet oils of poetry

eased it and light flooded in.
—'A Flowering Absence"

Yet it was this same, still at times hesitant voice that would be the first to create with courage and craft the local mythologies and experience of rural Catholic life in Ulster.

After completing his undergraduate education in Ireland, Montague returned to America in the 1950s, both as a student and as a Fulbright scholar, to study and write in workshops at Yale (1953-54), Indiana (1954), Iowa (1954-55), and Berkeley (1955). From this time comes his acid caricature of Senator Joseph McCarthy ("Visible Export," an epigram from a longer poem entitled "1953"), the nuclear haunted world of "Downtown, America" in which "TOTAL TERROR AND ECLIPSE" are "normal things and set the heart at rest," and the abstract world of "Field Theory," where "Ciphers of a new alphabet strain / Towards a magnetic nucleus of form." When he visits his aunt, Eileen Carney, in Queens and accompanies her to "our true Catholic / world, a graveyard" he sees his uncle's grave

>  and far from
>  our supposed home
>
>  I submit again
>  to stare soberly
>
>  at my own name
>  cut on a gravestone
>
>  & hear the creak
>  of a ghostly fiddle
>
>  filter through
>  American earth
>
>  the slow pride
>  of a lament.
>  —'A Graveyard in Queens'

In 1964 Montague returned to Berkeley as a teacher, where he came to know the "Bay Poets," especially Robert Duncan "in his Yeatsian cloak" and "the highly disciplined" Gary Snyder. "Some poems, even books" (like *The Rough Field*), he wrote to me in 1981, "would not have achieved their form if I had not met/read

Duncan, been friendly with Snyder, Ginsberg." Other influences and friends are given tributes in poems collected here: "William Carlos Williams, 1955" is remembered as he "stood on the Old / Capitol steps" at Iowa City; John Berryman, whom he first met in Iowa City, is recalled in "Ballad for Berryman;" and Theodore Roethke, whom he had first met in Ireland, is remembered in "Company." Montague's poems show that he knows the country as well as the poets. A sense of the vast continental expanse of America emerges in his famous love poem "All Legendary Obstacles," which recalls "the long imaginary plain, / The monstrous ruck of mountains." Indeed, Montague's America also includes Mexico (For "Death of a Chieftain" and "Coatlicue"), Toronto (for "Do Not Disturb"), and Vancouver Island ('Pacific Legend").

In the '70s and '80s, Montague has been a frequent visitor to America as a popular poet who has also been an especially prized teacher in Buffalo, Vermont, and, most recently, at SUNY Albany, where he holds the position of Distinguished Professor. His poem "Poetry Class" emerges from this experience in Albany. His papers are in the world-famous Poetry Room of SUNY at Buffalo, and he holds an honorary degree awarded by the State University College at Buffalo. Thus, it is especially appropriate that this book from Western New York should collect together the poems and stories that present John Montague's America.

This collection brings together thirty-seven poems (eight appearing in print for the first time), two essays, and three short stories (again with one appearing in print for the first time). Together they suggest the range of locale from Brooklyn to Chicago ("Talisman"), from New Haven to Iowa City, from Texas ("Bluegrass") to California, and the entire Canadian range from Toronto to Vancouver. In "Magic Carpet" (1988) Montague suggests this continuing span "from Cork to Upstate New York / from Altcloghfin to Albany." In an earlier, unpublished poem, "Sinnsear: Kindred" (1978), he can imagine himself walking with the fallen Kennedy brothers "through the epic landscape / of the Great Tain:"

> Footsteps of someone approaching
> by the sun-warmed gable of the barn
> caused Robert to turn,
> bending into shadow the still unbroken

>    column of his neck, as John
>    already had the back of his still shapely head.

If, as he suggests in that poem, "all mythologies are local, / courage related to time and place," we are particularly fortunate to have John Montague, a poet whose experience has made both of his worlds—the American and the Irish—local in his poetry and whose expression of heroics and ordinary human experience in the present and past can give us courage to face the extraordinary challenges of our ordinary world.

David Lampe<br>March 1991

# BORN IN BROOKLYN

## *THE FIGURE IN THE CAVE*

Young men (young women) ask about my "roots"
As if I were a *plant*...

I can't see it. Many are wanderers,
both Lawrences, Byron, & the better for it.
Many stay home forever: Hardy: fine.
Bother these bastards with their preconceptions...

I'd rather live in Venice or Kyoto,
except for the languages...
       (John Berryman, "Roots")

*"With all my circling a failure to return"* but to where? I was born in Brooklyn, St. Catherine's Hospital, Bushwick Avenue, in 1929, the year of the Depression. I returned there in the mid-1980s at the insistence of a journalist from *Newsday;* I feared to find the usual run-down brownstone. To my astonishment there was more left of the neighborhood than of Garvaghey. Yes, there was the local cinema with its matinée of monsters and Mickey Mouse. The wooden Indian was gone but one cannot expect one's childhood to be preserved, like a doll's house, or a Montague museum. And yes, there was the library, steps upward to a wide room full of books with, wonder of wonders, some of my own! And when I climbed the steps to the platform of the old El, I instinctively reached for a larger, taller hand. The trains must have been more sedate in my day, not scrawled with graffiti like action paintings,

but, as a sympathetic critic has suggested, "All Legendary Obstacles" could only have been written by someone whose infancy was full of the rumble of trains; likewise "The Cage" and "Last Journey."

And my first church was not Garvaghey chapel, where most of the Montagues lie buried, but a big Brooklyn church built by the dimes of Irish emigrants at the turn of the century. In its font I was baptized, fidgeted through mass with my family, until the funeral of my godfather, John Montague, bootlegger and quondam bush-league gangster. My Aunt Freda declares I got it all wrong in "The Country Fiddler" and that he would not be let off the boat in New York until he played a jig on the gangplank for the waiting crowd. I remember him as large-hatted, cheerful and kind, but I hear no music in the background. Instead the sound of many voices, sometimes quarrelling, the clink of glasses. And then the sounds die away because, without his help, we could not survive as a family. So my two elder brothers were sent home to the small town where they had been born, resuming their Fintona lives after only a five-year break in America. In Derry the children were shared out, and I went home with my aunt to become the last Montague, in the male line, to live in Garvaghey.

Garvaghey! I suppose that name is associated with mine, forever or nearly. I think of those few years from four to eleven as a blessing, a healing. My aunts wisely kept me at home for a year from school until I adapted to local ways, and no longer spoke of our Protestant neighbors, the Clarkes, as from the next block. I explored the mountain, roving farther and farther with my dogs, to the mass rock at Altamuskin where I stayed with Aunt Anne, or the endless slope of the Pole Hill, Slievemore, with its view as far as Monaghan. There was a hazel grove where the Lynchs and I cleared a secret meeting place and the little river where we guddled trout, bathed buck naked, raced or jumped in the meadow like the boy Fianna. When later I read the *Collected Wordsworth* of my Uncle Thomas, dated 1903, it all swam back. To visit Dove Cottage finally was like coming home to where another bewildered boy had lost and refound himself in nature, like an Indian brave.

\* \* \*

All this I seem to have been early aware of. I once wrote a playful variation on the usual child riddle:

> Who has a father, but is fatherless?
> Who has a mother, but is motherless?
> Who has brothers, but no family?

Myself, of course; losing a family and a country in one sweep must not have been easy, although for long I suppressed my earlier memories. The first proposition is probably at the root of my veneration for older writers of genius. I lost my letter of introduction to Ezra Pound in St. Elizabeth's and did not feel confident enough to call on Wallace Stevens at Hartford, but the year at Yale was very confused and lonely. I later sought out MacDiarmid, Robert Graves, David Jones, and already knew Austin Clarke—four masters concerned with the matter of these islands. Graves was also writing in a tradition of love poetry going back to the *armour courtois* which began here in the valley of Dordogne, a tradition in which I also inscribe myself, with modern hesitations. But I was always fond of my literary fathers, in verse and prose, and they have usually returned the compliment. In helping to get Kavanagh and Hewitt back into print I was also trying to recreate a context in which Irish poetry could flourish naturally once again.

The second proposition is at the heart of *The Dead Kingdom,* and probably most of my love poetry. The last has influenced my sense of literary comradeship: I like the French idea of a fertile literary community and would not wish anyone to go through what I endured as a young writer. The unselfish generosity of our great father figure, Yeats, seems to me an ideal that has been temporarily lost, but would Irish writing have world-wide respect but for him, serving as focus for both activity and reaction? From *The Dolmen Miscellany of Irish Writing* (1961) through my 1974 Faber anthology to *Bitter Harvest* (1989), the Scribners anthology, I have tried to present the best of my contemporaries. It is in this context that I find the element of self-seeking in the northern thing depressingly close to *Ulsterkampf,* when our giant forebears, Yeats and Joyce, have given us the freedom of the world.

And outside Ireland I belong to several interlocking groups of writers, quite naturally, the Irish branch, so to speak. I worked with the highly disciplined Snyder in Berkeley and at the weekends would ride pillion on his motorbike across the Bay Bridge into North Beach for a rich time of relaxation and reading. In Gian Carlo's, the San Francisco MacDaids, you might meet Jack Spicer, one of the first to cross linguistics and poetry, while Robert Duncan came sailing by in his Yeatsian cloak, his cast eye in a fine frenzy rolling. Was it luck or destiny that I walked in on a scene where poetry was briefly center stage, with electric public readings, often with music, jazz or Country Joe and the Fish. Robert had just published his great trilogy, *The Opening of the Field, Roots and Branches* and *The Bending of the Bow,* and his broodings on the neglected H.D. were ramifying into eternity. How curious it was to have gone as far as San Francisco to find someone who believed in magic like Yeats, and who persisted in the great romantic vision of Blake and Shelley!

Compared to the Mountain-Red and marijuana-fueled readings in the Bay Area, Paris has always taken poetry with mandarin concern. I find it strange that the flowering of French poetry in the twentieth century, with masters like Jouve, Char, Ponge, Michaux, Perse, has not been appreciated: a real anthology of modern French poetry would be staggering in its range. Again, I have been lucky in my contemporaries, beginning with Esteban who lived just across from me in the Rue Daguerre. I have translated many of them but they have repaid the compliment handsomely with a selected poems in French for my sixtieth birthday, translated by six poets. There is also a splendid selection from Bordeaux produced by a poet/publisher who calls himself William Blake & Co. If there are very few English among my friends it is, alas, because of the Little Englandism of the Amis generation. I have shared interests with Tomlinson, sparred with Davie, and feel I understand Hughes, but not since Auden has there been a talent which deploys the resources of the great English tradition which I once learnt, and now teach and read with passion.

An astonishing and heartening development is the way the American dimension is being restored to my life in my later years. If, as some psychiatrists argue, it is the first three years that are crucial, then a lot must have already happened to me before I was sent, following an old Tyrone tradition, into fosterage. I came upon a cache of letters once, dealing with those Depression years, written from Brooklyn by my Uncle John: it was a rough time. An old tabloid clipping describes how the family was rescued from being gassed by my eldest brother Seamus, coming home from school: the baby is described as still chortling in its cot. I have no doubt that the separation from my mother, whatever the reasons for the decision, is at the center of my emotional life, affecting my relationships with women, shadowing my powers of speech: my stammer broke out for the first time after she returned to Ireland. But though to understand, however dimly, is to begin to forgive, a writer should not forget, and my American past keeps surfacing. A journalist in the *Herald Tribune* turns pale on meeting me in a Paris bookshop; his father worked with mine on the New York subway, would cover for him when he went on the tear, rescue him, scoop him up, bring the Brooklyn equivalent of the wheel-barrow. "My mother was terrified of Jim's late night phone calls," said Charley Monaghan.

Brooklyn is dotted with people who share aspects of my early experience, including a poet Charles Martin, and I have always read people like Whitman and Crane with grateful recognition. And with American poets, like those I met in Iowa in the halcyon days of the Workshop, from Berryman to Dickey and Snodgrass, or much later in the releasing freedom of San Francisco in the sixties, with Snyder and Duncan and McClure, I have always felt a strong sense of kinship, the shared adventure of modern literature, to which Ireland has contributed so much as well. And yet I have been reluctant to stay there until now, taking the greenbacks without plumbing the responsibility involved. In 1956 I was stunned to see the Joyce manuscripts and portraits in Buffalo; now mine will be going to join them, as well as those of Graves, Dylan Thomas, and my dead friend Duncan: what more can I ask? With my first doctorate from SUNY followed by a reception from both houses of the New York State legislature, destiny seems to have decided to give me back my lost childhood in America just as my Tyrone background is being destroyed by bulldozer and bomb. Ballygawley is now as black a name as the South Bronx or Brooklyn.

It is like a fairy-tale, the little child who was sent away being received back with open arms. But while awed at the reappearance of this golden cradle to rock my dotage, I am grateful to have explored Ireland so intimately. Standing-stones and streams are not part of Brooklyn, nor are *cailleachs*. To judge by my contemporaries I would probably have been a writer, certainly a journalist, had I stayed in America. But who cut the long wound of poetry into my youth? Was it my mother who chose for her own good reasons to cast me off? She could have recuperated me when she returned, and I would have become as much a part of the fabric of northern life as my brothers in Fermanagh and Tyrone. But that would have been against my father's wish and I might never have really known the streaming hair of Aunt Brigid, praying nightly for us all. Or was it the strange figure whom everybody feared as a witch, but with whom I forged a real friendship? Speaking of my aunts she said, with a nearly Scottish burr: "They're trying to teach the wee boy to be a gentleman, like his grandfather, but where will that get him?" Women are everywhere in my work, healing and harassing presences, the other half of an equation one spends a lifetime trying to solve. I have been trying to put my love poems together and am daunted by the complexity of responses involved, from old woman to girl child.

Fragments of confession is a Goethean formula, and I approach my future with the energy of gratitude: what were once obstacles are becoming miracles, and after years of ploughing rough ground I might be allowed a period of harvesting. For a rearing can be too drastic, despite Kavanagh's theory about all art being "life squeezed through a repression." There was a time, seeking through the strange volumes scattered around Garvaghey, that I identified with the child martyrs, knives plunged in their proffered breasts. Henri Michaux describes how his imaginary tribe, Les Hacs, rear their artists "in an atmosphere of terror and mystery. . . the Hacs have arranged to rear every year a few child martyrs, whom they subject to harsh treatment and evident injustices." That dolorous discord, that forlorn note, still calls but something sustained me through those harsh, uncomprehending years. My amphibian position between North and South, my natural complicity in three cultures, American, Irish and French, with darts aside to Mexico, India, Italy or Canada, should seem natural enough in the late-twentieth century as man strives to reconcile local allegiances with the absolute necessity of developing a world consciousness to save us from the abyss. Earthed in Ireland, at ease in the world, weave the strands you're given.

It has been a golden autumn in Mauriac, the hamlet near St. Emilion where we now spend most of our holidays when we are not in West Cork. The *vendange,* or harvest the grape, is in progress, and great machines lumber between the rows of vines. It is a far cry from when I nearly passed out with the heat as I and my Derry friend snipped the champagne fruit. We worked all day and danced at the cafe in the evenings: now there is only one organized Fête, but a neighbor will pass in the evening with a basket of grapes and at the weekend we gather to taste the first fermentation. I feel at home here as I did in Garvaghey during the War years when I helped to work the farm, potatoes, bog, hay and corn. A neighbor passing in his tractor, a Massey-Ferguson, salutes me at my desk under the lime tree. His lifted hand could be the same salute as the new farmers in West Cork give me while I work in the garden of Letter Cottage: modern farming is as mechanized as warfare. But the mixture of respect and complicity in his greeting represents what I love in France, where to be an artist is only an extension of the normal: *"Bonjour, maître, ça marche, le boulot?"*

from *The Figure in the Cave*

## A MUDDY CUP

My mother
my mother's memories
of America;
a muddy cup
she refused to drink.

His landlady didn't know
my father was married
so who was the woman
landed on the doorstep
with grown sons

my elder brothers
lonely & lost
Father staggers back
from the speak-easy
for his stage-entrance;

the whole scene as
played by Boucicault
or Eugene O'Neill:
the shattering of
that early dream

but that didn't
lessen the anguish,
soften the pain, so
she laid into him
with the frying pan

till he caught her
by the two wrists,
*Molly, my love, if
you go on like this
you'll do yourself harm.*

And warmly under
a crumbling brownstone
roof in Brooklyn
to the clatter of
garbage cans

like a loving man
my father leant
on the joystick
& they were reconciled
made another child

a third son who
beats out this song
to celebrate the odours
that bubbled up
so rank & strong

from that muddy cup
my mother refused
to drink but kept
wrinkling her nose
in souvenir of

*(cops and robbers,
cigarstore Indians
& coal black niggers,
bathtub gin and
Jewish neighbors)*

Decades after
she had returned
to the hilly town
where she had been born,
a mother cat,

intent on safety,
dragging her first
batch of kittens back
to the familiar womb-warm
basket of home

(all but the runt,
the littlest one, whom
she gave to be fostered
in Garvaghey, seven miles away;
her husband's old home).


from *The Dead Kingdom*

## *MOTHER CAT*

The mother cat
opens her claws
like petals

bends her spine
to expose her
battery of tits

where her young
toothless snouts
screwed eyes

on which light
cuffs mild
paternal blows

jostle & cry
for position
except one

so boneless
& frail it
pulls down

air, not milk.
Wan little scut
you are already

set for death
never getting
a say against

the warm circle
of your mother's
breast, as she

arches voluptuously
in the pleasure
of giving life

to those who
claim it, bit-
ten navel cords

barely dried,
already fierce
at the trough.


from *A Slow Dance*

*A FLOWERING ABSENCE*

How can one make an absence flower,
lure a desert to sudden bloom?
Taut with terror, I rehearse a time
when I was taken from a sick room:
as before from your flayed womb.

And given away to be fostered
wherever charity could afford.
I came back, lichened with sores,
from the care of still poorer
immigrants, new washed from the hold.

I bless their unrecorded names,
whose need was greater than mine,
wet nurses from tenement darkness
giving suck for a time,
because their milk was plentiful

Or their own children gone.
They were the first to succour
that still terrible thirst of mine,
a thirst for love and knowledge,
to learn something of that time

Of confusion, poverty, absence.
Year by year, I track it down
intent for a hint of evidence,
seeking to manage the pain—
how a mother gave away her son.

I took the subway to the hospital
in darkest Brooklyn, to call
on the old nun who nursed you
through the travail of my birth
to come on another cold trail.

*Sister Virgilius, how strange!*
*She died, just before you came.*
*She was delirious, rambling of all*
*her old patients; she could well*
*have remembered your mother's name.*

Around the bulk of St. Catherine's
another wild, raunchier Brooklyn:
as tough a territory as I've known,
strutting young Puerto Rican hoods,
flash of blade, of bicycle chain.

Mother, my birth was the death
of your love life, the last man
to flutter near your tender womb:
a neonlit barsign winks off & on,
*motherfucka, thass your name.*

There is an absence, real as presence.
In the mornings I hear my daughter
chuckle, with runs of sudden joy.
Hurt, she rushes to her mother,
as I never could, a whining boy.

All roads wind backwards to it.
An unwanted child, a primal hurt.
I caught fever on the big boat
that brought us away from America
—away from my lost parents.

Surely my father loved me,
teaching me to croon, *Ragtime Cowboy*
*Joe, swaying in his saddle*
*as he sings,* as he did, drunkenly
dropping in from the speakeasy.

So I found myself shipped back
to his home, in an older country,
transported to a previous century,
where his sisters restored me,
natural love flowering around me.

And the hurt ran briefly underground
to break out in a schoolroom
where I was taunted by a mistress
who hunted me publicly down
to near speechlessness.

*So this is our brightest infant?*
*Where did he get that outlandish accent?*
*What do you expect, with no parents,*
*sent back from some American slum:*
*none of you are to speak like him!*

Stammer, impediment, stutter:
she had found my lode of shame,
and soon I could no longer utter
those magical words I had begun
to love, to dolphin delight in.

And not for two stumbling decades
would I manage to speak straight again.
Grounded for the second time
my tongue became a rusted hinge
until the sweet oils of poetry

eased it and light flooded in.


from *The Dead Kingdom*

## *THE LOCKET*

Sing a last song
for the lady who has gone,
fertile source of guilt and pain.
*The worst birth in the annals of Brooklyn,*
that was my cue to come on,
my first claim to fame.

Naturally, she longed for a girl,
and all my infant curls of brown
couldn't excuse my double blunder
coming out, both the wrong sex,
and the wrong way around.
Not readily forgiven,

So you never nursed me
and when all my father's songs
couldn't sweeten the lack of money,
*when poverty comes through the door
love flies up the chimney,*
your favorite saying,

Then you gave me away,
might never have known me,
if I had not cycled down
to court you like a young man,
teasingly untying your apron,
drinking by the fire, yarning

Of your wild, young days
which didn't last long, for you,
lovely Molly, the belle of your small town,
landed up mournful and chill
as the constant rain that lashes it,
wound into your cocoon of pain.

Standing in that same hallway,
*don't come again, you say, roughly,*
*I start to get fond of you, John,*
*and then you are up and gone;*
the harsh logic of a forlorn woman
resigned to being alone.

And still, mysterious blessing,
I never knew, until you were gone,
that, always around your neck,
you wore an oval locket
with an old picture in it,
of a child in Brooklyn.


from *The Dead Kingdom*

# *THE LETTERS*

That special silence of Sunday. All the family have gone to Mass. I listen to their steps fade down the road. There are no lorries on Sunday so sounds are clearer: I can hear the crows across in Lynch's plantation, the cows on the hill behind the house lowing to each other occasionally between mouthfuls of grass (there might be one looking the bull), the hens in the backyard, ceaselessly chatting about nothing, except one announcing the arrival of an egg. And my aunts' voices fading down the hill, every second fainter, as though down a well.

Did they really believe that I was sick? When Aunt Brigid entered the bedroom, I groaned and turned my face to the wall. "My stomach is hurting," I said, and managed a realistic hacking cough. I didn't really want to go to Mass; I liked the flowers on the alter, the bright vestments, but it seemed to go on so long: I would read the little bit there was in the Missal, or play with my beads, but there was always time left over, and shifting and staring at other people was supposed to be bad, especially when God was looking. And today was late Mass when Father Cush preached a long sermon, till everyone's knuckles were raw with cold. He had been to Rome last Easter, and could not stop talking about his visit; "as many statues as people."

So I groaned again, my face buried in the bedclothes. Aunt Brigid left the room and came hurrying back with a glass of white, foaming liquid. It tasted nasty but it was good in cause, so I drank it down while she watched me anxiously. "It must have been a cold he caught," I heard her telling Freda in the kitchen downstairs afterwards. "He'd better stay in bed a while till it clears. These cold mornings. . ." Freda grunted doubtfully but she didn't bother to climb the stairs and inspect me herself, as she might have done, if it had been a schoolday. I had never dared to stay away from Mass before.

So at long last I was alone, in the still-warm bed, which was far nicer than kneeling stiffly on a wooden bench, or fidgeting as Father Cush droned on. But in a few minutes I would be leaving this warmth to creak along the corridor, and down the stairs. For the real reason for my staying at home lay in a cupboard in the kitchen, a book which my cousin Kevin had left behind. I had watched him reading it while he was holidaying with us; had found it once lying, face upwards, on a chair, when he had gone for a walk as far as Clarke's, the Protestant farm up the road. There he would play the mouth organ, running up and down the keyboard with his head cocked sideways, while the whole family and their farmhands gaped at such lighthearted skills.

SEXTON BLAKE AND THE PEARL OF INDIA sang the tall letters on the cover. And underneath, in red, the subtitle screamed: *Our Famous Detective Fights the Devotees of the Goddess Kali— Another Thugee Mystery.* In the accompanying drawing a tall pale man in tropical clothes was being strangled slowly with a cord by a small brown man, perched like a monkey on his back. And above them shone a milky pearl, lighting the forehead of a mysterious lady with long dark hair and angry liquid eyes. How lovely she looked and yet how strange and violent the scene beneath her—at which she was smiling, like the Virgin Mary. I needed badly to discover what it was all about.

When Kevin left, at the end of his holiday, I hovered around to watch him pack. He wrapped his mouth organ carefully inside his pyjamas but he left the precious book behind. "Perhaps Johnny would like that," I heard him say, "though it might be a bit old for him." Aunt Freda looked at the cover dubiously, and turned it over. "I'll put it away for him," she said non-committally, "he has some comics at the moment." And I watched her pack it away at the back of the top left-hand drawer of the cupboard, the one where all the photographs and letters concerning family business were kept. Why was she putting it there, and how could they talk as if I were not present? I was sitting at the big table by the window, drawing with a crayon, and I heard and saw everything.

So in a way, the book was already mine, or would be, and I was not committing a sin I told the Infant of Prague on the bedroom table as I got up. And yet here I was tiptoeing like an Indian along the corridor, under the large smiling photographs of Uncle John who had owned this house but died in America. Why was I being so quiet? Houses where people used to live are mysterious, and these empty rooms were only peopled when my cousins came to stay. But a whole family had lived in them, not only my uncle and father (why was there no photograph of him?) but also my grandfather, whose old Bible, large as a flagstone, was in the smoky dark room over the fireplace. There was also a book about the American Civil War, full of illustrations, showing bearded men in slouch hats, carrying long rifles, or setting up their tents around a campfire. A famous photographer had taken them, sometimes endangering his life.

Each one of the stairs had a different squeak as I descended. Under the linoleum were copies of old papers which I had helped Aunt Freda to put down, so that we would have the pleasure of reading them in years to come. The death of Douglas Hyde was described in one, the All Ireland Football Final in another. And now I was in the silence of the kitchen, with the great black crook swinging over the fire, carrying its burden of black pots and thick-bellied kettles. They were planning to replace it with a stove but I loved the open fire where I could sit watching the flames as I dressed in the morning.

The cupboard drawer was too high for me to examine properly so I took the stool from the fire to enable me to look into it. There were several prayerbooks at the front and a wallet of photgraphs, most of which I had already seen. They were usually taken in the summer when my cousins were up from Longford and we went for a holiday to the seaside at Bundoran. And there was the Sexton Blake mystery, a thin volume neatly tucked in behind the photographs.

As I pulled it out I saw that there was a bundle of letters behind; a rubber band held them together. I could see from their length and color that they were foreign; the first one carried what I recognized as an American stamp, with the President's head, F.D.R. was he called? The handwriting looked familiar; could it be my father's? I had so few letters from him, and yet I was always longing for one of those blue envelopes with the big stamps. They were the only proof I had that I existed in the mind of a father I barely remembered seeing. Surely it would be right to have a look at them and find out a little more than my stray memories?

Now and again, dreamlike fragments of that American past rose in my memory. Wearing earmuffs against the fierce cold of a New York winter. Placing pennies—dimes wasn't it—on the shining trolley tracks. The tenement roofs of Brooklyn where one could play, peering down at the people far below: feeling small, I clung to the chimney stacks. A wooden Indian with headdress and tomahawk in the door of the cinema where we went to see Mickey Mouse. He scampering across the scene, squealing, while Minnie clattered after him in her big clogs. But there were less pleasant memories as well. The intense heat of summer, with water hydrants spouting in the street. The sound of voices raised in anger. I rolled back the band and opened the first thin sheet of what was not my father's writing but a large, fair hand like I know learnt at Gavarghey School.

*You asked me how are things going between the "couple." I wish you didn't because I'd rather not think about the whole thing. You know I don't think much of him and events have borne me out. He pulled up his socks after she came out and got a job in a grocery business but lost it because of some carelessness. They have a flat in a very rough neighborhood and they seem to quarrel all the time, since he is at home. He comes over to me looking for help but what can I do? He is my own brother but if I can work and drink, why not him?*

I stood trembling on the bare flagstones. <u>But it was not an ordinary cold I felt but something new to me, a kind of a weakening terror.</u> Was this the way grownups thought and spoke about each other? The oleographs of St. Francis looked down at me from the wall, a tiny army of robins and sparrows around his sandalled feet. A legend of pure love, our curate, Father Quigley called him. Should I read more? I took out the next letter in the series, looked at the thin light page.

*I gave Jim a job last week and we are all keeping our fingers crossed. You know the old story about the rat in the cheeseshop? Well, the point is that the poor rat set out to eat the lot and got sick after the first day and gave up cheese forever.*

*So I hope that working in a speakeasy will make him see what drink can do to people. I certainly wish it would do the same for me, though since I have to keep things going, I keep my head pretty steady. Strange how these years have been so good for me when bad for most people. Funny how I fell on my feet in New York doing what our father disapproved of back home, making poteen, that is. Hooch they call it, though we do it differently here. We use the bath, which is always full. So we have to go next door to the MacGarrity's, to wash, which the children find funny. They are living with me, now, on the top floor. I forgot to say that the reason I gave him the job is that she is pregnant again, a get-together after one of their quarrels, I suppose.*

The letter had a lengthy P.S.

*If she weren't so hard on him, I think he might hold out better. But they squabble like tinkers, and she is much sharper than him, dainty though she seems. The last time she was banging him around the head with a saucepan—it was a funny scene—shouting: "You're no good, like the rest of your family." When she caught sight of me she had the good grace to go red with embarassment. She told me—privately as she says—that she married the wrong man. And I must say that when she's angry she looks pretty with her big eyes, and her hair astray. But I find women more trouble than they are worth, though not you two, of course, sisters are different. The baby is due next February, I think.*

In a kind of dream, like sleep walking, I skipped through the little packet, to open the very last one: the datemark was several years later, 1932.

*I hope you won the law case about the right-of-way to the bog on the top mountain. Anything to do with the law is always so tricky, though I think I got the details right on the map I drew for you. It was quite funny to sit here trying to get the details of bogroads, gates, and the length of bogbanks right, over here in Brooklyn. I couldn't help wishing I was up on the Coal Hill, that warm wind on my face. Shall I never see Tyrone again?*

*I regret to say that I have bad news to report from here. Molly is sick again. In fact she has not been really well since the birth. I must say Jim is marvelous with the baby. To see him crooning to it (he still sings quite well) makes me like him all over again. As its godfather, I am concerned about it and wonder what will happen to this new John "Junior," as they say here. I do my best for them but I have not been feeling well myself lately, and there are plans to change the drink laws which would close down my business. I told him that if anything happened to me he should think about sending them all home again.*

Finally I understood, standing there with the letters in my hand. I felt cold again, colder than I had ever been. My stomach began to heave, with small, dry sobs. But there wasn't that much time, and things had to be tidied up. Still queasy, but determined, I began to rearrange the letters, one after the other, according to their postmarks and snapped the rubber band round them before slipping them back, behind the lurid cover of the Sexton Blake, which I now did not care if I ever read.

Across the creaking house then, past my Uncle John's photograph, past the Infant of Prague, I crept, back to bed. I was still shivering but eventually I fell, or cried, myself to sleep.

The special silence of Sundays. I awake to the footsteps coming back up the broad road. The sound of voices, without hearing the words, meaningless as gulls crying over fresh ploughland. Gravel grating under a foot, a key grating in the door. "I hope he's alright," my older aunt's anxious voice.

He will never be the same again and it is partly his own fault. Those who pry learn what they deserve.

*(1991)*

# THE COMPLEX FATE OF BEING AMERICAN-IRISH

For the title of this brief essay I have borrowed from Henry James, that famous grandson of South Ulster, who having defined the complex fate of being American, spent a large part of his life trying to escape the problem, in France and England. I think I know a little of his dilemma, as a Brooklyn-born Ulsterman with an Irish domicile, but I would be more inclined to stress the potential richness, even the comedy, of such contradictions, as well as the creative anguish.

For instance, was Henry James not also an Irish man, if not an Irish writer? Under the most recent rulings for Irish citizenship he would pass, because of his grandfather. William James left about 1789, an emigrant from the now disputed Border area of Ulster. Had political events anything to do with his emigration? Tom Flanagan might know, as part of his heritage is from the same area. But certainly the wind of history was blowing around his Calvinist coattails, as they would be again for his family, if they had stayed.

But to be more literary, is his grandson's intense sense of evil in any way to be attributed to his Northern Irish heritage? That is the kind of speculation which is beautifully endless, perhaps ultimately useless, the kind of debate one might hope to have in some celestial barroom. But I have a few more puzzling imponderables to add. The family of Poe were neighbors, as the crow flies, over in Ballyconnell. And if there is any area of Ireland with a haunted reputation it is nearby Moy Slacht, the plain of slaughter, where blood sacrifice may have been practiced.

> Here was raised
> a tall idol of savage fights:
> the Cromm Cruaich—
> the King Idol of Erin.
> —from the *Book of Leinster*

So do the maelstrom of Poe and *The Turn of the Screw* owe anything to those dark, small hills? There is also the fascinating fact that one of the most powerful traditions of supernatural writing is Anglo-Irish, from Sheridan le Fanu to Bram Stoker. So could we inscribe Poe and the darker side of Henry James in the long line of guilt-ridden Protestants, afraid of the face at the window?

But to return to my own case history. I have known in my own life and work the complex fate of being American-Irish, or Irish-American, whichever way you wish to lay the emphasis. Thomas Wolfe wrote that only the dead know Brooklyn but I was born there, in Bushwick Avenue Hospital in 1929, a combination of time and place that will need no explanation to this audience.

So I played on a tenement roof, put nickels under the subway trains, gaped at the cigarstore Indian in front of the local cinema, spread the Funnies across the floor on Sunday, knew Dick Tracy and Orphan Annie before I saw the Beano. I went to the pictures to see Mickey Mouse and Buck Rogers with my brothers and was pulled through the snow on a curved sleigh by my father. What would have been my future if I had stayed? Again there is that desperate story of Henry James, "The Jolly Corner," about the man who returns. Somewhere in New York my *alter ego,* my *doppelganger,* sits brooding over his destiny; would I have become a distinguished American professor, Kevin Flanagan, Tom Sullivan, David Casey, Tom Greene? Or a different kind of Doctor, lynchpin of this society? How would I have woven together my two worlds, the New World and the lost Ireland?

Or to raise the ante, what would Dev have become, if he had stayed: Cardinal or Chief of Police? Of such accidents is a destiny made. Instead, de Valera and I endured emigration in reverse; we were returned to the old sod, the mother country, or, in my case, the lost green field, that truncated part of Ulster known as the Six Counties. In both cases it was simple poverty: there was no way that my parents could bring up their children in what seemed, certainly to my mother, "a wild and threatening world of Prohibition and Depression, cops and robbers, cigarstore Indians and coal-black niggers, bathtub gin and Wop neighbors."

So at the age of four I found myself back on a decaying farm in Tyrone, the heartland of Ulster, unwittingly the inheritor of three nationalities, for the post office van that came to our door in the mornings was bright red, Royal Mail. How did I cope? My aunt Freda tells of how I used to speak of visiting my Protestant neighbors as "going to the next block." What the Clarkes thought of that little boy in knickerbockers I don't know but one day I came back late and declared that I had "been kepping the cows."

That day the language of Ulster poetry took a minute step forward. My early poems were attempts to do justice to that world I had returned to, its Scotch, Irish speech patterns, its long history. I had moved back from the twentieth century to at least two thousand years before Christ, the strange signs on the stones of Seskilgreen and Knockmany, or Cnoc Aine, the hill of the Mother Goddess whose saddle shape dominated our little valley where old-style farming still lingered on, and would linger until the tractor drove out the horse, and hens were put into concentration camps.

And yet I have kept a double vision, a part of me still profoundly moved by my American *patria,* my American heritage. In *The Rough Field* there is a section called "The Fault," which seeks to explain the pain of my father, a dispossessed Ulster Republican whose only secure job was as a nickel-pusher on the I.R.T.:

> Often as I descend
> into subway or underground
> I see his bald head behind
> the bars of the small booth;
> the mark of an old car
> accident beating on his
> ghostly forehead

But there was also my mother who loathed Brooklyn and would not, could not stay. Her main criticism of *The Rough Field* was that it said nothing about her family. It is an irony that the closest relatives I have left in New York, the Carneys, are from what we would call the North, her side of the house. I have a poem called "A Graveyard in Queens" about the grave where my godfather and namesake, John Montague, rests beside her brother, Thomas Carney. My uncle John was a musician and as I stood there I seemed to

> hear the creak
> of a ghostly fiddle
> filter through
> American earth
> the slow price
> of a lament.

And in my next long poem, *The Dead Kingdom,* I described her marriage, part of which was lived under the shadow of the Brooklyn Bridge, that splendid dream in steel whose centenary we celebrate this year (1983). Someday I will put all my American poems together, to suggest the complex fate of being an Irish-American. One I am especially proud of is "All Legendary Obstacles," a love poem set against the background of western America.

> All legendary obstacles lay between
> Us, the long imaginary plain,
> The monstrous ruck of mountains
> And, swinging across the night,
> Flooding the Sacramento, San Joaquin,
> The hissing drift of winter rain.

Why, I demand grumpily, is this not to be found in any American anthology? Is it because I am supposed to be only Irish? Modern poetry used to be a common adventure, above national prejudice; Joyce and Yeats appear in the *Pisan Cantos* of Ezra Pound. And here I must stress another line of exchange between our two countries. Some American artists still feel a specific pull towards Ireland, in particular two of the best poets of recent times. When I brought Ted Roethke to meet Mrs. Yeats it was clearly a major event in his life although It was hardly fair of him to demand that his wife Beatrice should immediately become a medium. And John Berryman chose to end his *Dream Songs* in Dublin, declaring of Yeats, "I have come to have it out with you Majestic shade." I deal with these two strange pilgrims in another forthcoming book but I would like to end with a final comic touch about being American-Irish. If the borough of Brooklyn ever decides to recognize me as a lost poetic son they will not have to go to any trouble to honor me, for there is already a Montague Street. Whatever about their royalties neither Norman Mailer nor William Styron can claim as much!

*(1983)*

## THE COUNTRY FIDDLER

My uncle played the fiddle—more elegantly the violin—
A favourite at barn and cross-roads dance,
He knew *The Sailor's Bonnet* and *The Fowling Piece.*

Bachelor head of a house full of sisters,
Runner of poor racehorses, spendthrift,
He left for the New World in an old disgrace.

He left his fiddle in the rafters
When he sailed, never played afterwards;
A rural art silenced in the discord of Brooklyn.

A heavily-built man, tranquil-eyed as an ox,
He ran a wild speakeasy, and died of it.
During the depression many dossed in his cellar.

I attended his funeral in the Church of the Redemption,
Then, unexpected successor, reversed time
To return where he had been born.

During my schooldays the fiddle rusted
(The bridge fell away, the catgut snapped)
Reduced to a plaything stinking of stale rosin.

The country people asked if I also had music
(All the family had had) but the fiddle was in pieces
And the rafters remade, before I discovered my craft.

Twenty years afterwards, I saw the church again,
And promised to remember my burly godfather
And his rural craft, after this fashion:

So succession passes, through strangest hands.

from *A Chosen Light*

## *STELE FOR A NORTHERN REPUBLICAN*

Once again, with creased forehead
and trembling hands, my father calls
me from stifling darkness....
Little enough I know of your struggle,
although you come to me more and more,
free of that heavy body armour
you tried to dissolve with alcohol,
a pale face straining in dream light
like a fish's belly
                upward to life.
Hesitantly, I trace your part in
the holy war to restore our country,
slipping from home to smoke
an absentee's mansion, concoct
ambushes. Games turned serious
when the cross-fire at Falban
riddled the tender of policemen,
one bleeding badly
                stretched upon
the stone flags of our kitchen,
your sisters moving in a whisper
of blood and bandages. Strange war
when the patrol scouted bales
of fodder, stray timber, tar
to prepare those sheltering walls
for reprisal's savage flames
if he should die!
                That night
you booked into a Strabane hotel.
"Locals were rarely used for jobs:
orders of the Dublin organizer,
shot afterwards, by his own side."
A generation later, the only sign
of your parochial struggle was
when the plough rooted rusty guns,
dull bayonets, in some rushy glen
for us to play with.
                Although again
and again, the dregs of disillusion

churned in our Northern parents' guts
to set their children's teeth on edge;
my mother hobbling to the shed
to burn the Free State uniforms
her two brothers had thrown off
(frugal, she saved the buttons):
my father, home from the boat at Cobh,
staring in pale anger at a Redmond
Commemoration stamp
                  or tearing to
flitters the polite Masscard sent
by a Catholic policeman. But what if
you have no country to set before Christ,
only a broken province? No parades,
fierce medals, will mark Tyrone's re-birth,
betrayed by both South and North;
so lie still, difficult old man,
you were right to choose a Brooklyn slum
rather than a half-life in this
by-passed and dying place.

from *The Rough Field*

## *THE FAULT*

When I am angry, sick or tired
A line on my forehead pulses,
The line on my left temple
Opened by an old car accident.
My father had the same scar
In the same place, as if
The same fault ran through
Us both: anger, impatience,
A stress born of violence.


from *The Rough Field*

## THE CAGE

My father, the least happy
man I have known. His face
retained the pallor
of those who work underground:
the lost years in Brooklyn
listening to a subway
shudder the earth.

But a traditional Irishman
who (released from his grille
in the Clark Street I.R.T.)
drank neat whiskey until
he reached the only element
he felt at home in
any longer: brute oblivion.

And yet picked himself
up, most mornings,
to march down the street
extending his smile
to all sides of the good,
(all-white) neighbourhood
belled by St. Teresa's church.

When he came back
we walked together
across fields of Garvaghey
to see hawthorn on the summer
hedges, as though
he had never left;
a bend of the road

which still sheltered
primroses. But we
did not smile in
the shared complicity
of a dream, for when
weary Odysseus returns
Telemachus should leave.

Often as I descend
into subway or underground
I see his bald head behind
the bars of the small booth;
the mark of an old car
accident beating on his
ghostly forehead


from *The Rough Field*

## A CHRISTMAS CARD

Christmas in Brooklyn,
the old El flashes by.
A man plods along pulling
his three sons on a sleigh;
soon his whole family
will vanish away.

My long lost father
trudging home through
this strange, cold city,
its whirling snows,
unemployed and angry
living off charity.

Finding a home only
in brother John's speakeasy.
Beneath the stoup
a flare of revelry.
And yet you found time
to croon to your last son,

Dear father, a gracenote.
That Christmas, you did
find a job, guarding a
hole in the navy yard.
Elated, you celebrated
so well, you fell in.

Not a model father.
*I was only happy
when I was drunk*
you said, years later,
building a fire in
a room I was working in.

Still, you soldiered on
all those years alone in
a Brooklyn boarding house
without your family
until the job was done;
and then limped home.


from *The Dead Kingdom*

# *THE OKLAHOMA KID*

It was my Cowboy period. On the fringe of the newly ploughed field behind our house I practiced my draw, with two sticks peeled and whittled to revolver shape. There was the simple hip draw, like Buck Jones, thumbs resting on the belt, fingers crisply spread, like eagle's talons. Then as your opponent moved (batted an eye nervously, before slapping leather), the releasing plunge downward to action. A double explosion—Bang, Bang!—and a thistle fell dead, in the full pride of its pale, prickly life. The daisies shook their sunbonnet heads in dismay while all other thistles moved (despite their roots) a step backwards: The Oklahoma Kid was in charge.

Then there was the border cross draw, hands flat across the stomach, relaxed but dangerous as serpents. A cow moved its flank to shudder off a fly and the serpents uncoiled. Twin mouths of flame flickered in the air, gunsmoke and cordite (I did not know they were irreconcilable) drifting across the spring grass.

Tim, our farm horse, watched me, a green scum of grass on his protruding lower lip and wedge-shaped teeth. I renamed him Thunder and rode to town, his flanks glistening with sweat, his glove-deep nostrils pulsing as he heaved for breath. Unconcerned, he lashed his tail, dropped his head to lip in a daisy, and I saw the harness marks on his neck, the sagging belly roped with veins, and felt oddly ashamed. A smell of clover, the drone of a bee away into silence, and the prairies of my imagination—long grass of Wyoming, red-rock mesa of Arizona—dwindled to a boy in dungarees standing in a field in County Tyrone; Northern Ireland to some,

Ulster to others. Hearing my aunt call I raced in, tamely: someone was looking for me in the shop.

Every day, the country people came down the mountain roads to our house. Some came punctually to collect their pensions, for it was a sub-Post Office, and one of my aunts was postmistress. White-haired, gaunt as a rake, she stood in her little office among the weighing scales and postal regulations, indicating where X his or her mark should go. Others came to buy odds and ends, liquorice allsorts, Paris buns, MacLean's Headache Powders from what had been, in my grandfather's time, a flourishing shop and to which they were still attached by strands of loyalty. One family came—one or other of seven identical children, lugging a basket as big as himself across the fields—because they had quarrelled with the new grocer, an entirely new and more up-to-date business, half a mile down the road.

These were the usual callers, bound by no regulation (though the post-office was supposed to close at 3 p.m.) except weather and the rhythm of work on the land. A dry day in winter, a wet in summer presented equal opportunities but, generally, they preferred to come at twilight, thus saving labor and light. Which is why I remember the shop as a scene by La Tour, the people standing well back in the shadows, my aunt's white head bent close to a grease-spattered candle, a smell of damp clothes, bread, cream of tartar, pervasive as the smell of paint in a studio. They loved her, unjudging audience of all their troubles, but they wore her out.

During the winter, we had another group of callers: those who came to borrow books. For our house was also a branch of the Tyrone County (Carnegie) Library and my other aunt was Honorary Librarian. As she was often occupied around the farm, I was consulted as Deputy Librarian. Already, at ten, I was a formidable bookworm, imagination sprouting in isolation like one of those sickly potato stalks one finds in cellars. A hundred books came each quarter, arranged in wooden cases with hasps like pirate trunks. Sixty fiction, twenty juvenile and twenty general knowledge and by the end of a month I would be familiar with the contents of some and the titles of all, and able to advise with authority. Ranged on the half-empty shelves, they soon smelt like all the other commodities, faintly sweet and musty, with patterns of damp on the bindings.

The main demand was for fiction. At school, few of the older children read, plunging directly into the work of the farm when they came home. So the Juveniles lay unused except for my predatory dismissal. And General Knowledge meant little to the people of the district, speculative only about local things. Even books on farming, with their background of hops, cider and Harvest Festivals seemed far removed from life on the soggy hillfarms of Tyrone. So it was fiction they sought, to fill the long hours of the winter nights. And fiction consisted of only two kinds, Love Stories and Cowboys.

The Love Stories were my aunt's domain. A reader herself, she sampled them before passing them on, and not only for pleasure. Many of the farmers' wives read, but the most voracious were two large ladies, one seventy and one fifty, one single and one married, alike only in their unslakeable thirst for that mysterious thing called Romance. If my aunt was out, she would have left a selection aside, which I would pass over the counter, primed for the moral discussion which seemed inextricable from Love Stories.

"Is there any Love in it?" they asked, peering at the title doubtfully in the poor light. Ruby M. Ayres, Isobel C. Clarke, Annie S. Swan, Ethel M. Dell—how I remember those romantic sounding names! And the titles, *A Stranger to Paradise, The Primrose Path, An Open Heart,* wicket gates to a world where slender, flowering English girls called Penelope or Millicent awaited the dreamlike destiny of love. No one found it strange that, like the books on farming, they should always deal with settings completely foreign to us: books were like that, a province of the unreal.

"Your aunt said the last was good, but there was damn all love in it."

"There's plenty this time," I said, hedging furiously.

"Is it good love or the other sort?"

"The other sort," that vice to which love stories were prone, was beyond me, but I could parrot a testimony. With childish cunning I saw that what they deplored, they secretly coveted: the questioning was a necessary moral front.

"It's mostly good," I said, "but there's a doubtful bit at the end."

When the choice came to be made, however, the questionable book generally went into the basket, joining the Inglis Pan loaf, the pot of Richhill jam, the Andrew's Liver Salts. I had no illusions about love stories: in any case, I was delighted to be accepted in complicity in an adult mystery. But my capacity to corrupt was limited: the really questionable books, the ones entirely devoted to love of the wrong sort, had already been locked away by my far-seeing aunt.

With the Cowboy stories I came into my own. I had only recently graduated from Juveniles (the face of the prince suddenly shaded by a sombrero, the witch changing her broomstick for a rustler's pinto) and for a time the charm of mere killing was enough. But I was in search of more than the elementary violence of the Wild West Club, and when I discovered my first Zane Grey, I knew I was in for a long ride. It was *Riders of the Purple Sage,* and when the boulder rolled down, sealing off the Mormon family in the valley, I quivered with excitement. I asked Mr. Ferguson the post-van driver, who spent the day in a little hut at the end of our turfshed (it was the end of his thirty-mile run) before driving back in the afternoon to head-office, whether Zane Grey had written many books. He said that he had seen in the paper once that Zane Grey was a woman and that she had written over a hundred books, many of them posthumous. This information puzzled but pleased me: a hundred books would take a long time to read.

I can see now that the hallucinatory hold these stories gained on me was because I connected them with a mysterious previous life. Every six months or so, Mr. Ferguson brought long blue envelopes bearing flamboyant stamps to remind me that I had an existence elsewhere in the mind of a father, who had sent me back, during the Depression, to the only place where he had been happy. How was I to know that Arizona was nearly a continent away from Bushwich Avenue, Brooklyn, where only cigarstore Indians were to be seen, and that in fostering my dream I was cancelling that of my father?

My circle of fellow-readers was small but intense. Besides Mr. Ferguson (who hardly qualified since I saw him only on Saturdays when I was free from school), there was a dark-jowled young man called Dan Lynch, who lived with his mother and sister on one of the most remote farms under the shadow of Coal Hill. With his hat crushed on his head, he would swing in onto the gravel before the house and leap from his bicycle as though from a lathered horse. Henry Anderson, on the other hand, was a gaunt Presbyterian farmer who demanded my advice gravely before making his choice. If Dan was the typical hardjawed cowboy, Henry Anderson was the Mormon preacher or sheriff, just, severe, taciturn. When he gave back the book, it was generally wrapped in a page from *The Farmer and Stockbreeder* upon which he had laboriously noted the words he could not understand. Hugh Kelly, who drove Gormley's lorry around the back lanes, made a fourth. There were others, like John Mooney, our serving man, who read an occasional book, but these were the cream of the outfit.

To these rather quiet, hard-working men, my childish insistence was at first strange, then amusing. Cowboy stories had been for them a recreation after a hard day's work, but I demanded more. Before passing out a book I would give a judgment and expect one in return. If there were too many people in the house, we talked by the roadside, turning over pages by the light of a hissing carbide bicycle lamp. The incongruity of the scene did not strike us: briefly we shared the illusion of a wider world, with electric storms crackling over the prairies, stampeding the wild horses. Was that the sound of hooves on the Belfast road?

One thing did trouble me, although I was afraid to speak of it. We were all agreed that Zane Grey was the best. Although Clarence Mulford and W.C. Tuttle were also good, they lacked the authentic detail of *Wildfire* and *West of the Pecos*. But there was such a lot about women in some of Zane Grey (perhaps he was one after all?) who were often discovered without their denim shirts, a warm flush mantling neck and bosom. This was all right if the hero was involved, because he had the shyness of chivalry, but when, in one story, a vicious outlaw kept a woman chained in a cave, I was dismayed: the Cowboy stories seemed to be following the Love stories. That the scene filled me with a new feeling, at once hot and guilty, dismayed me even more: was I turning outlaw? I finally showed the book to my aunt who took a brief glance at it and put it away, without comment. But what was so fascinating about naked women? Whipping my imaginary mustang as I drove the cows home from the hill pastures in the evening, I wished I knew the answer.

My great sadness, however, was that, as the winter ended, the work of the fields slowly reclaimed my cowboy friends. First it was the ploughing. Coming home from school, I would see another field opened and wave to a figure on a headland, turning with his team. Then, as the days lengthened, there was the sowing; when the oats were in, I would be staying at home a few days to help with the cutting and planting of the seed potatoes. In the meantime, people read still, but more slowly, taking as much as a month to finish a book. Soon they would stop reading altogether.

It was then that I heard about the film. Someone had seen in the local market town a poster announcing the coming of *The Greatest Cowboy Film of All Time—The Oklahoma Kid*. I had been to a few films (each year a visiting priest showed slides of Mission work on a sheet in the local hall) but this was different, and not to be missed. After dinner, I ran out to bring the news to my fellow-readers where they were working in the fields. Henry Anderson was gathering dried potato stalks and burning them by the riverside.

"What do you think we should do?" I asked.

He threw another gripful of stalks on the pyre, which fumed a grey-black smoke.

"I'll have to talk to the others," he said, slowly. "But if it is as good as you say, I think we should go."

Several nights later, at the end of the week, we met at the crossroads to discuss the situation. Henry, as the eldest, led the conversation, proposing that we should club together and hire Gormley's Hackney.

"How much would that be?" asked Dan Lynch anxiously.

"Gormley generally charges two quid for the run, but he'd give it to me for less," said Hugh, with an expert's smooth knowledge. "Not counting the cub here, that makes about ten shillings a skull."

Although the sum was far beyond my savings, I was decided not to relinquish my equality.

"I'll pay for myself," I said, with defiance.

"If the nadger pays that makes a four-way split; are you game?"

We all looked at Dan. Despite his habitual cheerfulness, everyone knew that he found it a hard struggle to support his mother and sister on the tiny farm and that he rarely had pocket money, even for cigarettes. Nevertheless we could not offer him a loan, however well meant, because it would indicate that we knew his plight, and reticence in money matters was one of the facts of the countryside.

"If you can find a fifth man," Dan said finally, "I'm game."

For the following week, we talked of little or nothing but the film. According to Hugh Kelly, the principal part was taken by an actor who had been a cowboy himself, and the whole thing would be authentic, down to the last cowclap. Even the taciturnity of Henry Anderson dissoved before such golden possibilities: "It might be a real good night," he said. As for myself, I rehearsed the scene daily after school in the fields behind the house. It would be the first time I had ever gone to town, on my own account, without a watchful relative.

It was not until the evening we left that I learned who was to be the extra man. They had canvassed several people, including casual readers like John Mooney, but all said they had neither money nor time for such a foolish jaunt at a busy time of year. There was one man in the parish, however, who was well known never to refuse a chance for an outing, however long or for whatever purpose. In despair, therefore, they asked Papa (short for Peter Anthony) Cummins.

Papa was a smallish, rather dusty-looking man who always sported a green hat with a large chicken feather stuck under the band; together with his mottled complexion, it made him look an aging Indian brave. This, however, was the only relevant thing about him, from our point of view, because he openly scorned books, all the more so since his wife was one of the two romance addicts. His chosen activites were card-playing—he was a deadly hand at twenty-five, the favorite game in the district—and above all, talking. From morning till night his flow of chatter went on, ceaseless and indiscriminate as a river down which floated anything, dead dogs, cornstalks, old turds. Seeing him approach, people doubled on their tracks, disappeared under bridges, vanished in a cloud of pipesmoke, but he was still there when they reappeared, a bucket or spade tucked jauntily under his arm, his nasal voice grinding away at their wits.

My own uneasiness where Papa was concerned was simple: his outspokenness troubled me. Generally, country people never talked much about themselves. But Papa recognized none of this reticence, speaking of his wife, for instance, as casually as though she were something he had picked up at the Hiring Fair. His conversation was spiked with jokes and innuendoes, which by the subdued guffaws that greeted them, I guessed to be somehow connected with the Love stories. My prudish altar-boy's soul was both fascinated and revolted.

But there was a further reason. As I grew older, the strangeness of my situation troubled me increasingly: not only could I scarcely remember my life in America, but I could hardly even remember my father. With the indifference of the hardworked, my aunts did not speak much of the past and failed to understand my secret pleas for information. My main hope lay then in what casual knowledge I could find. Patient as an archaeologist, I reconstituted the past from old books and photographs and the rambling conversation of the older men in the parish. The image of my father I got was vague but flattering, that of a red-haired young man who sang occasionally at dances and was a demon for practical jokes. Only Papa among the men of my father's generation refused to answer my questions and I sensed he disapproved. Once when someone, in the way of adults, placed his hand on my head and asked what I was going to be when I grew up, he rounded sharply, before I could speak, and said with a rough emphasis I have never forgotten:

"He'll probably be blackguard, like his father before him."

At the crossroads, that evening, Papa was the first to arrive. Typically enough he had not changed, his hands stuck in the pockets of his overalls, a newly cut ashplant under one armpit. The others had washed after coming in from the fields, their faces shone a scrubbed red and they had on soft Sunday shoes. When Hugh appeared with the car, his arm dangling self-consciously through the driver's window, the group was complete. It was a big Vauxhall and we all piled in, Papa in front and the three of us in the back.

The whole journey was dominated by the whine of Papa's voice. Henry and Dan sat on either side of me, their hands square on their knees. It had been a damp day and the landscape had that stereoscopic brightness that sometimes comes after rain, or just before twilight. On either side, men were still working in the fields. My companions should have been delighted with his chance to observe the methods and progress of others, but they seemed stricken with self-consciousness. Only Papa kept his eyes open, delivering a running commentary as we passed: "That's good even plowing now," or, "The man drove that furrow should be shot."

Outside Strulebridge, where the river curled under a grey bridge, there was one field sloping directly into the sun, in which the green shoots of an early crop were just beginning to appear. A sight like this was so rare that I expected a comment, but all my companions did, when Papa drew their attention to it, was to knead their caps slowly, nodding assent to his admiring: "There's a right snappy farmer for you!" What was wrong with them, and why were things not going as I had expected?

Soon we were at the outskirts of the town, the wealthy well-tended grounds of large private houses, the golf course with its striding pylons. Laganbridge, a sturdy market center with about eight thousand population, was ten miles or so from my home. I was brought to it twice or three times a year on shopping expeditions, and its main street, dominated by the Courthouse and the War Memorial, was my only real image of urban life, contrasting with my half-memories of America. As we turned in the Belfast road, I felt a familiar excitement, all the sharper because I was now entering for the first time as an equal among adults. There was the long low shape of the County Library, the center from which all our books came. Above it appeared the twin-spired silhouette of the Diocesan Cathedral, with the college in its shadow to which I might be going in a year or two. All these details seemed to fuse into a mysterious and seductive whole promising something subtly different from the pace of the farm. My awareness of Papa's presence diminished: the Oklahoma Kid was finally coming to town.

There was a further dimension to this new and potent image: the town was nervous with change. This was spring 1940, and through Main Street paraded a detachment of British soldiers. We stopped the car at the foot of the courthouse to let them pass. First came a tall man wearing a busby and leopard skin, his eyes fixed fiercely ahead, runnels of sweat coursing down his jaw. Then drummers, left legs dragging with the weight of their instruments, upon which they gave an occasional marching pace rattle. Then pipers, in kilt and cloak, with white mouth-pieces resting on their shoulders. Behind was the rank and file, in sober khaki, polished boots clattering, arms rising and falling like puppets. Under the sand-bagged courthouse they marched, out the Barracks Road, and in the distance we heard the band strike up again at the drum-major's harsh command. Its sudden flourish shot a shiver down my spine.

We were not the only ones to have stopped to watch. Along the pavement was a thin line of people, still in attitudes of listening. Some seemed countrymen, like ourselves, their inexperience betrayed by their weighty pose. A few customers had emerged from the shops, packages in hand; there were even one or two shopkeepers, wearing their white aprons. But most of the onlookers were girls, of every shape, size and age, their eyes bright, their lips wounded with lipstick.

"There's no shortage of women about here," said Papa, appreciatively, looking around him.

In order to be in time for the film, we had agreed that it was better not to eat at home but to have something in town. After a hurried fish-and-chips in Danielli's, we made our way toward the cinema—it was the smallest of the three in town—which lay through a maze of sidestreets. Our pace was slow, because the pavements were clogged with people. At first, we took for granted that they were shoppers, but, as we elbowed our way in single file, it gradually dawned on us that they were mainly soldiers. Of various ranks and regiments (thick serge of the Inniskillings, black berets of the tank corps, light blue of the R.A.F.), they pushed their way along, obviously at ease and at home. And when we finally got to the cinema, we found them again, a large queue of fighting men and their girls, stretching straight down the street and round the corner. Five sheepish Oklahoma Kids come to a twentieth-century town, we stood looking on: there was not the remotest hope of getting in.

It was as we were making our way despondently back to the car that Hugh suggested that perhaps we would have a chance of getting into the new cinema. This magnificent building, a concrete palace called the Coliseum, stood right in the center of Main Street, between Littlewood's and Woolworth's. Ordinarily, it would never have occurred to us to try such a place, which had the reputation of being very expensive, and was frequented mainly by townspeople. There was added reason for suspicion which my companions understood but I did not. Run up by a local contractor to cater to the new trade brought by the war, it was decorated in the Arabian Nights style, with spangles and stars on the ceiling and double love-seats at the back. These latter had brought down the wrath of Canon Kerr, the fiery old administrator of St. John's, who described them in an Easter sermon as "hot seats to Hell."

Now, however, the Coliseum seemed the ideal solution. In the discreet, carpet-heavy hall, a queue was filing, supervised by a splendid commissionaire in sky-blue uniform and cap. It was a long queue, but unlike the tin-roofed cinema at the end of town, the atmosphere was orderly and the rate of absorption regular. Fenced by plush ropes, we waited, stolid as oxen, whiling away the time by looking at publicity stills or testing the carpets in which, as Papa said, one could sink to the fetlocks. Finally, the commissionaire came over to us:

"Two first," he said. "Main film's begun."

"What's that?" asked Henry anxiously."

"He means we'll have to separate," Hugh explained.

"I'll take the laddy," said Papa promptly. "Where do we go now?"

Bumping through the darkness after the cinema attendant's torch, we found ourselves going down the vast shelving floor of the auditorium. Every row seemed filled, a sea of dark heads. Nearer and nearer loomed the screen until the usherette led the way across in front of it. As we followed, I saw a tiny box-shaped shadow rising and falling at the bottom of the screen: it was Papa's hat. At the far corner, underneath the double sign EXIT/GENTLEMEN, were two empty places. Seats banged as we sat down. "They don't give you much room for your legs," commented Papa, turning himself several times, like a dog, before settling.

Directly above us, high and insubstantial as cloud formations, reared the images of the film. A window opened like a gulf at the back of a modern apartment to reveal a vista of skyscrapers. A man crossed the screen, his legs, distorted by the angle of vision, grasshopper long. He was speaking angrily to a woman whose face suddenly swam up to us in close-up: beautiful, sad and as huge as a barn door.

"God," said Papa, "That's the living spit of young Barney Owen's wife. But I didn't know she wore make-up."

In a street now, a yellow taxi speeding through the bright lights of the city.

"What's happening?" demanded Papa impatiently rapping his ashplant against my legs. "Where are we going?"

It was only then that the truth homed on me. Despite his travelling, Papa had never been to the cinema. His journeys were in search of new listeners, not new sights, and once set down, he continued talking. I remembered with sudden horror a story of how he had gone with a party to the All-Ireland in Dublin and spent the day in a relative's house in Clontarf, listening to the game on the radio. This was the first time he had ever been in a picture house, the first time, indeed he had ever been affronted by the idea of fiction. What he thought was happening on the screen, whether he regarded these images as real people or shadows, I could not say, since he struck straight through it to whatever everyday life he could recognize.

A man came hurrying down to greet the couple and bring them back through the stage-door.

"That fellow has a wee look of Micky Boyle about the eyes," Papa announced.

"S-sh," came from behind us, the first indication that we had an audience.

Inside the theater, some kind of rehearsal was in progress. Stagehands were moving in the shadows, shifting scenery, focusing lights. Standing with the couple in the wings, we saw the soprano spotlighted on the stage, her throat distended with sound, her bosoms rising and falling.

"She has the right big udder," said Papa admiringly.

The comment behind us had risen to an uproar. "Disgusting," I heard several times as I tried to sink lower in my seat.

As the singer spread her arms in one final throbbing note, a chorus came tumbling out onto the stage, drum majorettes wearing cartwheel cowboy hats and boots, and kicking their long white legs in the air. Papa leaned forward so as to inspect them more closely.

"Where did you say we were?" he asked.

"In New York—in America," I said, my face flaming.

"By Jasus, they don't wear much in your country. Bare legs and big diddies!"

It was this remark, delivered at the top of his voice, which finally provoked an intervention. From the row behind a soldier thrust his closely cropped head between us.

"Look 'ere, Grandad," he said mildly, "you're not the only one in this dump."

For the first time, Papa became aware of his audience, but without understanding how he had gathered it.

"What the hell's wrong with you?" he said sharply to the head which had landed so unexpectedly in his lap.

"Put a cork in it, will you, please," said the soldier with patient exasperation. And then, seeing that Papa still did not understand: "Would you mind closing up?"

"Shut up yourself," said Papa angrily, "or I'll give you a belt."

He raised his ashplant in the air: wavy as a spider it appeared on the screen, right across the face of the leading man.

That did it. Cries of protest came from every part of the house, including the balcony. Several people rose in their seats, craning to see what was happening, while the commissionaire raced down the aisle, shining his torch directly into Papa's face.

"I'm afraid you'll have to leave, sir, you're creating a disturbance."

"What hell disturbance do you mean?" said Papa. "I'm danged comfortable. And the wee fellow's great: he's explaining it all to me."

"People are complaining."

"That's right," said a hard voice. "Put him out."

"Come on," I said, tugging at Papa's coat. "We'd better leave." But I don't think he would have gone except that our three companions suddenly appeared beside us, having heard the row from the other side of the hall.

"I think we'd better go," said Henry Anderson, gravely.

Everyone turned to watch as we marched out, Papa in front, escorted by the commissionaire, myself last, thankful for the darkness which hid my face. At the door, the manager was waiting, a plump little man who hovered around us in dismay.

"There's never been anything like this here before. But we'll refund you your money if you insist."

But Papa had understood finally and was disgusted.

"You can shove your auld cinema up your ass," he said sharply, and jamming his hat down on his head, led us out onto the pavement.

I remember one more thing about that evening in Laganbridge. As we passed glumly down the street, a group of boys were standing outside the sliding door of Lyons garage. Several of them wore boiler suits. They watched us with interest and before we were out of earshot, one of them gave a low incredulous whistle.

"That's a right crowd of country-looking idiots," he said. I looked at my companions. If they had heard him, they did not betray it by the flicker of an eye. Dark-faced and silent, they plunged down the street towards the car.

By right, the story ends there, and anything further will only spoil it. During the return journey, Papa sat at the back and Henry in the front. I don't know what they talked of, or indeed, whether they talked at all, because I soon fell asleep with my head sideways in Papa's lap, from which I had to be lifted when I got home.

But life often adds a postscript; seventeen years later, I descended from a Greyhound bus in Oklahoma City. In the glaring cafeteria, the voice of Elvis Presley was wolfing through "Heartbreak Hotel." Gene Fullmer had just beaten Robinson: the paper I had bought in Salt Lake City the previous night was full of it, since Fullmer was a local man. Eating a sour mess of beef and hash, I began a conversation with the man beside me. He seemed rather disreputable, his hat jammed on his head, his jaws masticating ceaselessly. Yet he also seemed somehow familiar— that great nose, that coppery tint (noticeable even under a day-old beard), those wise eyes of legend.

"I'm a Cherokee from Tulsa," he said, with what I took to be both fatalism and pride. "What part of Oklahoma do you come from?"

"From Oklahoma City," I said, involuntarily, "County Tyrone," and choked with a mixture of joy, shame and ridiculous conceit.

from *Death Of A Chieftain*

## RESPECT

Thady, sixty years out of Donegal,
propped, overflowing his tall barstool,
my father's pal, the last, hollering:

"Jim was a decent man, he prayed every night
for his family; I'm glad to meet his son.
Sure, he took the drop, but never gave in."

(They shared a horsebox in a Brooklyn slum,
a boarding house run by rheumatic Mrs. Averril
who pitted her rosary against the Atom Bomb.)

"But your uncle was a right whoremaster,
riding black women." Monaghan's father
snorts in the background, "Keep the party clean."

Just as our ears were beginning to burn!
Thady, an old motor man, reverses gears,
rewinding the thread of those solitary years

To recall a summer evening in Donegal,
how he won the raffle in the Parish Hall.
First prize: a kiss from the prettiest girl.

His eyes moisten, his voice thickens,
he lays aside his daily, *Journal American,*
"I can still picture her shy expression."

Among gasoline fumes, run-down brownstones,
Thady still holds on to his lucky number,
waiting stolidly on the platform beside her,

How when he kissed her, there was a cheer.
"The one time in my whole life." Thoughtfully,
Thady looks back down into his chilled beer.

"But I have always respected women.
So did your father." The stale odor
of lives broken down, next to nothing,

yet, on the litter, that stray offering.

from *Mount Eagle*

## *A GRAVEYARD IN QUEENS*
### *for Eileen Carney*

We hesitate along
flower encumbered

avenues of the dead;
Greek, Puerto-Rican,

Italian Irish—
(our true Catholic

world, a graveyard)
but a squirrel

dances us to it
through the water

sprinklered grass,
collapsing wreaths,

& taller than you
by half, lately from

that hidden village
where you were born

I sway with you
in a sad, awkward

dance of pain
over the grave of

my uncle & namesake—
the country fiddler—

& the grave of almost
all your life held,

your husband & son
all three sheltering

under the same
squat, grey stone.

    \*

You would cry out
against what has

happened, such
heedless hurt,

had you the harsh
nature for it

(swelling the North
wind with groans,

curses, imprecations
against heaven's will)

but your mind is
a humble house, a

soft light burning
beneath the holy

picture, the image
of the seven times

wounded heart of
her, whose portion

is to endure. For
there is no end

to pain, nor of
love to match it

& I remember Anne
meekest of my aunts

rocking & praying
in her empty room.

Oh, the absurdity
of grief in that

doll's house, all
the chair legs sawn

to nurse dead children:
love's museum!

    \*

It sent me down
to the millstream

to spy upon a
mournful waterhen

shushing her young
along the autumn

flood, as seriously
as a policeman and

after scampering
along, the proud

plumed squirrel
now halts, to stand

at the border
of this grave plot

serious, still,
a small ornament

holding something
a nut, a leaf—

like an offering
inside its paws.

*

For an instant
you smile to see

his antics, then
bend to tidy

flowers, gravel
like any woman

making a bed,
arranging a room,

over what were
your darlings' heads

and far from
our supposed home

I submit again
to stare soberly

at my own name
cut on a gravestone

& hear the creak
of a ghostly fiddle

filter through
American earth

the slow pride
of a lament.


from *A Slow Dance*

## DOWNTOWN, AMERICA

The car wipers work against the fretful snow
NEWS OF THE LATEST TRIAL—THE WINNING HORSE—
TROOPS HAVE LANDED—COMMISSION'S REPORT IS
    THROUGH
These are normal things and set the heart at rest.

Buy a bargain in a Big Sale store,
Careful that the salesgirl does not gyp you, though:
With purchases come walking through the snow:
These are normal things and set the heart at rest.

Snow grants grace to an industrial town
Formation of crystals on the dingy ground;
The distant bass of Long Island Sound:
These are normal things and set the heart at rest.

The car radio suggests our new form of fear,
TOTAL TERROR AND ECLIPSE ARE HERE—
ATOMIC MUSHROOMS MAY FLOWER ANYWHERE—
But these are normal things and set the heart at rest.


from *Forms of Exile*


## VISIBLE EXPORT

On the white screen, his powdered jowls,
all the gutter talk & malice of Dail Eireann
cunning pig eyes—an Irish politician
ranting and raving, ransacking the mystery
of other people's lives—McCarthy: un-American.


(from *1953*)

## CULTURAL CENTER

### Room I

Consider here the various ways of man:
The central crucifix from which the rigid figure
Hangs, minatory and Catalan;
The robust contours of an imperial brow
Nose bridge spanned according to a law,
With lips that barely condescend to form a kiss
(Since Roman virtue is chief end on earth
And desire sufficient without spirit's rebirth);
While in a corner the Indian God
With multiplying hands, makes strange appeal
For concord, even in a place crowded
And wild with views as this:
His is a sort of benign and universal kiss.

### Room II

Through corridors, in juxtaposed grace
Conflicting modes assume their permanence.
This lady has the pure Renaissance face
Of a Botticelli virgin in vernal radiance;
This tapestry has birds that lift their wings
In gestures of freedom from the woven silk.
How lightly the Japanese mountain rests its weight,
as though not intending to offend the earth!
And all this delicacy confronts, affronts,
The stark and staring crucifix.

### Room III

Europe is dying, these motions say,
With this sharp body twisted all awry,
These diagrams in horror from a burnt out city,
A canvas sprawling like a battlefield, with slaughtered forms,
While bright and clear, subduing all,
A complete abstraction judges us,
From its clean white wall.

### MAIN HALL

A tiny nun is leading her whole class
Of chattering girls, through buildings

Perfectly constructed from pure glass,
To where this version of her vision stands:
At her corded waist swings
A minute harmless god of silver plate,
Until at last, inoffensive, starched and mild,
She stands possessively beneath
No tinselled Christmas suburb child,
But the lean, accusing, Catalan crucifix.

from *Forms of Exile*

## AMERICAN LANDSCAPES

### I—GHOST TOWN

A loud-speaker car drones through the streets,
Calling JOIN THE U.S. MARINES.
The road winds past a bone-white church
To emptied mounds, abandoned mines of gold.
Where husky madmen scrabbled for wealth,
Lurching through desert streets to bars
And the gaudy shacks of Madame La Boulette,
Now stray cats prowl and tourists follow signs.

### II—BUS STOP IN NEVADA

The blind, the halt, the lame descend these steps.
This cheapest form of transport gets its trade
From God's worst handiwork, the botched and poorly paid
In a land of honey. The anaemic lady,
The bloated shop girl rush into desert sunlight,
Blazing a trail of comic books and smoke
To where, in a sullen cafeteria,
Percolators hiss and cheap pies line the glass.
Hands ply the glittering cranks of slot machines
Seeking catharsis in a deluge of coins.
Beyond, the snow-capped Sierras bluntly rise:
Travellers raise their bored and famished eyes
To where bright snow and forest limn the weightless skies.

### III—HOLLYWOOD AND VINE

In the evening, the wide-shouldered boys
Tight black jeans, leather jackets springing free,
Stalk through the drugstored streets
Turning cold faces under the lights,
And call, on an urge of shrillness,
To girls stuttering past, aloof on high heels.
Lost in rising gales of laughter,
In their own awkwardness suddenly angular,
They answer with a forced look back,
Pivoting nervously to the cats' call of love.

from *Forms of Exile*

## *EARTHBOUND*

I—NEWSREEL

Four suave and public men, in braided uniforms,
Devise, like portly knights, a table round:
Chivalric with medals and winking cross they seek
A delicately devious path to common ground.

They come to cut a continent up,
To carve a suppliant country, or advise
The briefest way to end hostilities:
A dead age deadens in their Kodak eyes.

Into the past sail silhouetted battleships,
The cigar-like tubular grace of the zeppelin,
As before cutlass and spear,
The centaur skill of cavalrymen.

Anonymous men trample sodden ground,
Repeat their bravery before the speaking guns,
While, like a stealing valley mist,
Blue poison gas corrupts the lungs.

Softly swords rust in warriors' hands,
As into dust sigh obsolete machineries:
These stout and changeling fathers mime,
Like constant ghosts, our grail-like destinies.

from *Poison Lands*

## II—FIELD THEORY

True work, Lawrence cried, not aesthetics!
And, like Ghandi, praised the hand-weaver,
The subtle, natural skill of Navaho or Hindu,
Whose patterns are vivid with their life.

But our world is increasingly abstract:
The soundproof room in the high glass building
Where the Cabinet weave through statistics
The pattern of their nation's development;

Or the pallid face of Oppenheimer
Confronting a formula on the blackboard,
Schrodinger's Wave Equation, perhaps,
The simplicity of its complexity, absurd.

Daily we tend in a systematic direction
Developing mental skills, until work
Becomes detached and pitiless as chess,
Permutated with purely neural grace.

Still in some of this new analytic wisdom
An old madness prevails. The thin smile
Of Hammerskjold masking a passion for poetry,
The head of Einstein, a shabby, pacifist lion:

As the artificial planets blossom
Into the gravitational field of the sun
Ciphers of a new alphabet strain
Towards a magnetic nucleus of form.

*(1954)*

## III—EARTHBOUND
### *for Robin Skelton*

In the sleeping
head of the world
a light clicks
& a male insect
with metal legs
creaks down to a
stricken surface;
earthbound, we
share our ghostly
emissaries dance
through gravity,
but the pale-faced
imperious virgin
who rules our best
dreams still strides
the night, a skirt of
clouds at her waist,
a bola of stars
to herd, to goad
her attendant tides.

from *Tides*

## DO NOT DISTURB

A lift rising towards
or falling from, love.
Caressing glances, dart-
ing, possessive touches;
the porter's conspiracy,
distaste of the outraged.

That always strange moment
when the clothes peel away
(bark from an unknown tree)
with, not a blessing moon,
but a city's panelled skyline;
an early warning system

Before, disentangling,
through rain's soft swish,
the muted horns of taxis,
whirl of police or fire engine,
habitual sounds of loneliness
resume the mind again.


from *The Great Cloak*

## *GONE*

I awake to dawn in a strange
place, hearing the birds acclaim
repetition with their light voices,
a defiant pattern of beauty
flagrant as the heavy blossoms
hanging wet against my window.

But ornate magnolia, Belle of Portugal
rose with its outlandish whiteness,
the grey-blue musk of eucalyptus,
seem only to stress, in a need
born of their resolute gaudiness,
one overriding fact: your absence.

from *The Great Cloak*

## *TALISMAN*

After talking together
we move, as by a natural
progress, to make love.
Slant afternoon light

on the bed, the unlatched
window, scattered sheets
are part of a pattern
hastening towards memory

as you give yourself
to me with a cry of
joy, not hunger, while
I receive the gift

in ease, not raw desire
& all the superstructure
of the city outside—
twenty iron floors

of hotel dropping
to where the late sun
strikes the shield of
the lake, its chill towers—

are elements in a slowly
developing dream, a talisman
of calm, to invoke against
unease, to invoke against harm.


from *The Great Cloak*

## *ALL LEGENDARY OBSTACLES*

All legendary obstacles lay between
Us, the long imaginary plain,
The monstrous ruck of mountains
And, swinging across the night,
Flooding the Sacramento, San Joaquin,
The hissing drift of winter rain.

All day I waited, shifting
Nervously from station to bar
As I saw another train sail
By, the San Francisco Chief or
Golden Gate, water dripping
From great flanged wheels.

At midnight you came, pale
Above the negro porter's lamp.
I was too blind with rain
And doubt to speak, but
Reached from the platform
until our chilled hands met.

You had been travelling for days
With an old lady, who marked
A neat circle on the glass
With her glove, to watch us
Move into the wet darkness
Kissing, still unable to speak.

from *A Chosen Light*

## WILLIAM CARLOS WILLIAMS, 1955

After a reading where
you had been made
fun of, teased
and prodded (not
the milkless Olympian
bull of your poem),

you stood on the Old
Capitol steps, looking
at the neat stars
and when I spoke
you put your arm
around me saying

*"poet, poet!"*
From anyone else
it would have been
ridiculous, but you
made the gesture
(of manumission, almost)

seem so instinct-
ively natural
that I am still
trying to live up to it,
learning to answer
to *"poet, poet?"*


from *A Chosen Light*

## *DEATH OF A CHIEFTAIN*

Revolver in one hand, machete in the other, his T-shirt moist with sweat (except where the raft of the sun hat kept a circle of white about his shoulders), he beat his way through the jungle around San Antonio. Behind him followed a retinue of *peons,* tangle-haired, liquid-eyed, carrying the inevitable burden of impedimenta. With their slow pace, their resigned gestures, they seemed less like human beings than like a column of ants, winding its way patiently over and around obstacles.

When they came to a clearing that satisfied him, he declared a halt, calling up his carriers in succession. The first put down the table he had been hugging across his shoulders, peering through its front legs for the path ahead. Around the table were piled various instruments and items of food with, to top the mound, a bottle of *tequila* and a neat six-pack of Budweiser beer. With the air of an acolyte bringing a ritual to its conclusion the last carrier approached, lugging a battered cane-chair. Bernard Corunna Coote sat down, breathing heavily.

Food, first. Like a bear let loose in a tuckshop, he ransacked the parcels, tearing the tinfoil or polythene bags open. Half an hour later, while the natives lay around, somnolent as stones after their brief meal of *tacos,* he was still fighting his way through a cold roast chicken, washed down by draughts of lukewarm beer. Wiping his mouth, he turned to work.

Compass and sextant, lovingly consulted, pinpointing his position. Then he erected a triangular instrument, like a theodolite, and took readings, both horizontal and vertical. As though satisfied of where he stood, but not what he stood on, he produced a gleaming spade and began to sink holes around the clearing. From them he took "samples," handfuls of red clay and stone, which he heaped on the table, to the height of a child's sandcastle.

By the time he was finished, the whole clearing looked as if it had been attacked by a regiment of moles. From under their conical hats the Indians watched: now it was their turn. Exasperated by their sleepy gaze, he dispatched runners into the forest to bring back further samples. When they returned to lay their spoils before him (curiously shaped fragments of flint, stones faintly resembling arrowheads, stones in which veins of mica flashed) he interrogated them about anything they might have seen, with an optimism that only gradually died into disappointment.

All these details were entered on a large roll-like map of the district. At the top of the chart, in a fair hand, was inscribed the Indian name of the region: *Coatlicue,* the land of the Goddess of Death. At the bottom was the owner's name: *Bernard Corunna Coote, His Property.* In between from the central axis of San Antonio, the ever increasing lines of his excursions radiated outwards, like a spider's web.

If the center of the spider's web was San Antonio; the center of San Antonio, as far as Bernard Corunna Coote was concerned, was the Hotel Darien. It stood on a promontory overlooking the town, a great bathtub of a building whose peeling façade was only partly disguised by a fringe of palm trees. The disparity between its size and the adobe hovels gathered around its base would have been shocking, were it not for its enormously dilapidated appearance, like a rogue mosque. From whatever angle one approached, its grey dome was the first thing to become visible; a landmark to the market-going Indian, slumped on his burro, a surprise to the traveller, who felt as though he were arriving at Penn Station or St. Pancras.

The history of the Hotel Darien combined mercantile greed with the despairing quality of romance. In the 1890s, after the failure of the de Lesseps Panama project, a group of Liverpool and New York businessmen (already linked by the golden chain of considerable shipping profits) had been taken by the idea of cutting a railroad through the jungles of Central America. Such a railway would save ships the dangerous journey round Cape Horn: cargo could be shipped across the isthmus in a day. The tiny fishing villages at either end would become great ports, where the goods of half a continent were transferred from boat to rail and vice-versa. And so the Hotel Darien came into existence, a luxury hotel where top-hatted businessmen could relax, gazing prorietorially out onto the Pacific.

And then, in 1902, while the first cowcatcher was pushing its way through the jungle, news came that the United States had taken over the Panama Canal project. The Hotel Darien did not die immediately: one does not destroy a white elephant if it has been sufficiently expensive to construct. The railway came in due course and though the opening was less spectacular than planned (il Presidente's speech was drowned in a tropical thunderstorm) there was a little light traffic, especially tourists attracted by the idea of travelling through savage country, with a stout pane of glass between them and the alligators. But it degenerated into a jungle local, staggering from village to village, its opulent carriages white with bird-droppings.

Business picked up slightly in the 1920s with the planning of the Pan-American Highway. But even that passed about fifty miles away and only occasional parties deviated to San Antonio, drawn by the legend of the railway or by the few excavated archaeological remains in the area. Gradually the Hotel Darien sank to what seemed its place in the scheme of things, a remote limbo for remittance men, unwanted third sons, minor criminals, all those whose need for solitude was greater than their fear of boredom. And strays from nowhere that anyone had ever heard of, like Bernard Corunna Coote.

Bernard Corunna Coote came to San Antonio in the late summer of 1950, part of a guided tour from Boston. He looked out of place from the beginning, a large man, sweating it out in baggy flannels and tweed coat, with, perched incongruously on his forehead (like a snowcap on a tropical peak), the remains of a cricketer's cap. He stank of drink and had the edgy motions of someone who had not slept for days: black circles were packed under his eyes.

His companions skirted him as they descended from the bus. Only one person showed any interest in his arrival: from his niche under a pillar on the shady side of the square, Hautmoc, the town drunkard, opened an opportunistic eye. When the American matrons chattered off, armed with cameras, in search of the colorful town market, Hautmoc moved in. He found Bernard Corunna Coote sitting on the terrace of the town café, drinking *tequila.*

"Señor he said, with sweeping politeness, "may I join you?"

When the main party of SUNLITE TOURS returned, Hautmoc and his companion were still deep in conversation. Originally spotted as a soft touch, something in the uneasy bulk of his victim had moved Hautmoc, who was busily explaining to him his favorite subject: the ethnological basis of American civilization. His mahogany face, mystical with drink, leaned towards the white man.

"But in the mountains, beyond the Spaniards' reach, the poor people remained," he oracled. "They—we—I are still a pure race."

Coote did not speak, but his eyes flickered interest.

"Spaniards, bah? a decadent syphilitic race from a dead continent. Mexicans, bah! a spawn of half-breeds. The true Indian . . ."

The SUNLITE TOURS bus was loading in the square. As the negro courier looked over, sounding his klaxon, his passenger ordered another *tequila.*

"You were saying?" he asked.

"The true Indian, *los hombres de la sierra,* are the aristocrats of this hemisphere, the purest people in the world."

The courier came towards them, touching his hand to his yellow SUNLITE cap.

"Mr. Coote, we're leaving now, sir."

Bernard Corunna Coote turned up a watery, but firm, eye. "I have just discovered the purest people in the western world," he said in Spanish. "In such circumstances, one does not leave. *Yo me quedo aqui.*"

As the bus roared from the square, a surprised line of New England matrons saw their late travelling companion and an unknown Indian, their two heads together, roaring with laughter. Between them, like a third party, stood the new bottle of *tequila.*

"In the old days," said Hautmoc, with a meaningful gesture towards the bus, "we would have sacrificed them. A land must be irrigated with blood!"

And thus Bernard Corunna Coote became one of the permanent guests of the Hotel Darien, and as much a feature of the town in his own way as Hautmoc. Daily he padded down to the square for a morning drink, and to collect his mail. According to the postmaster, a quiet student of these matters, most of the letters bore a king's head and came from Inglaterra. But there was also a newspaper bearing the ugliest stamps he had ever seen, a pale hand clutching a phallic sword, and surrounded by what looked like (but was not, as he found when he consulted the dictionary) Old German script. It was all mildly puzzling, and he took the unusual step of being polite to Hautmoc when he next met him, hinting at a free drink if information was forthcoming. But as everyone had long ago agreed, the latter was a cracked vessel, returning little or no sound, except his pet theories about race and human sacrifice.

"I don't know," he said, screwing his eyes like an animal dragged into the light. "*Es muy dificil*. He says he is from the oldest civilization in Europe, as old as the Indian. But it is not English."

To the rest of the town he was *el Señor Doctor*, the brooding figure whose place at the café table no one ever took, even on market days. The schoolboy cap had given way to a wide-brimmed sun hat, the tweed coat had disappeared, he wore floppy cotton drawers, and rope-soled sandals instead of Oxfords, but they could still recognize a learned man when they saw one. Even if mad: catching those large, watery eyes upon them the women in the market-place drew their rebozos over their heads and made a gesture of expiation as they bent to ruffle among their baskets of fruit and pottery.

II

The people in a position to know most about *el Señor Doctor* were those who appeared to care least: the three other permanent guests of the Hotel Darien. The oldest was not really a guest, being the hotel manager, but he had so little work to do (and that he tended to leave to the servants) that only rarely were his companions reminded of their business relationship with him. The cadaverous Iowan, called Mitchell Witchbourne, his bony features had the ascetism of a Grant Wood painting: one looked behind him, expecting to see a clapboard barn and silo. This impression of weathered starkness was increased by his high-pitched voice. Night and day it creaked, like a weather-vane, sending out stories, jokes, hints of what looked like hope and communication, but gradually took on the shrillness of signals of distress. At forty he had been manager of a chain of Mid-Western hotels, from Chicago to Colorado: what had brought him, ten years later, to a decaying seaport on the Pacific coast?

No one knew either what had brought Jean Tarrou, the neatly moustached little Frenchman who spoke English with a slurred brokenness which grew more charming each year. A devotee of *la culture physique,* his room was full of mechanical contraptions upon which he practiced nightly. (An American matron, hearing the sounds from the adjoining room, had burst indignantly in to find him squatting in black tights on the carpet, one hand held high, the other pointing sideways, a human semaphore. His legs were caught up in pulleys, towards the ceiling, at an angle of 45 degrees.) Now and again he dropped hints of a distinguished past, a *licence ès-lettres* from the Sorbonne, consular service in the West Indies, but the trail came to an abrupt end with the last war. He had served under Vichy, but did not detest de Gaulle, a paradox which indicated that his troubles were as much private as political. In any case, like most French people, he did not discuss matters with people outside his family circle, even when, as in San Antonio, they were either far away, or non-existent.

The person about whom most was known was Carlos Turbida, who was still young enough to derive satisfaction from the idea of being a black sheep. The son of a wealthy Mexican fish merchant, his father had retired him from the capital after his third paternity suit (it was not the behavior he objected to, but the carelessness). Officially, he was in charge of the south-west section of the family fishing fleet, and, once a week, he roared away in his Porsche to the nearby harbor. Tarrou had seen him there, the distinctive olive-green machine parked among the fishing nets while a bored captain pretended to listen, as he strutted up and down the quay. He even cultivated a sailor's walk, but the effect was not so much athletic as sexual: he rolled his hips as though carrying a gun. But generally he lay in bed, eating sweets, reading movie magazines, and dreaming of Acapulco: the perfect portrait of the Latin-American *cicisbeo.*

Their main interest in Coote was mathematical: he made the necessary fourth for most card games, poker, bridge, gin rummy. To endure the silence of a placc like San Antonio, habit was indispensable. Five evenings a week they played, grouped around a table on the veranda, while the tropical night grew heavy outside, and the Indian waiter came, bringing a lamp, and fresh drinks. At first they played for *pesos,* but then, disdaining the effort of tossing coins on the baize, they turned to counters, using matchsticks as chips. As the sums involved mounted—from tens they progressed to hundreds and sometimes thousands—even that kind of tally became impossible. So each time the soberest of them (it was usually Tarrou) kept a record. Though their skills were equal, it was necessary, to keep an edge on the game, to believe in some apocalyptic day of reckoning: in the meantime, there was the drug of ritual contest, with memory floating to the surface as the hands were occupied.

"I remember once," said Turbida, "driving from Monterey to Mexico City. You know the road?" He raised two fingers to indicate a bid.

"Up, up, up," said Witchbourne, sawing an imaginary steering wheel. "Then, down, down, down." He clutched his stomach.

"I spent the night in a little hotel, high up in the Sierra Madre. In the corridor, outside my room, I see the, how you say, chambermaid. She has long black hair, down her back, a pure Huastecan Indian. As she pass, I take hold of it."

"I pass," said Tarrou, and posed his pencil over the white slip of paper at his side.

"Let me go, she cries, let me go. There were tears in her eyes. I say, I let you go, if you come back to stay. That night, I sleep with her six times. She cries again when I leave in the morning. What can you do with silly girls like that?"

"You can only eat them," said Tarrou, pleasantly.

"I'll see you," said Coote, hunching his shoulders across the table towards Turbida. The latter laid down his hand calmly: in the heart of his palm two dark queens lay, without embarrassment, beside two smiling red knaves.

"Damn," said Coote.

There was silence while Tarrou shuffled the cards, laying them (with that pendantic precision he brought to every action) in a neat semi-circle before each man. If Turbida's stories were mainly sexual, his were more frightening, tasteful vignettes of people and places which only gradually revealed, under their smooth surface, an underlying terror.

"It is on that route, if I remember rightly," he said, "that the natives bring one glasses of freshly crushed orange juice. The bus stops by the groves just at midnight and the whole air is full of the smell of oranges."

Both Witchbourne and Coote reached simultaneously for more whiskey.

"But it is not quite as gracious a custom as on the route to Vera Cruz," he continued. "There is a little station there, just before the railway descends from the mountains, where the women come, selling camellias laid out in hollow canes, like little coffins. It is only then that one notices that most of the women are crippled: one has no fingers, another no nose, a third a stump instead of a leg."

"Heredo-syphilis," said Witchbourne gruffly, "the Spanish pox. These mountain villages, no water, no medical services, intermarriage: never get rid of it." His moustache was bright with whiskey.

"I bid you a hundred pesos."

"I raise you fifty," said Turbida excitedly.

As Coote threw in his hand, Tarrou leaned forward, delicately poised as a cat. "I will raise you both fifty," he stated. After a further flurry of bids, the others faltered, throwing in their hands. While Tarrou recorded his victory, Witchbourne swept up the cards for the next deal, glancing swiftly at the Frenchman's as he did so: three fours.

Of Witchbourne's conversation there was little to be said: the past for him was a devastated territory, a no-man's-land, through which he wandered, picking up fragments. Hardly anything he said could be added to anything else, the only recurrent factor being his practice of ending the evening by telling a joke. And his favorite was the story of *The Vicar and his Ass*. When he began, everyone tensed, assuming stares of interest, like executives on a board meeting.

"There was a parish in the mountains where the people had a long way to go to church. So they all went on their asses, and to pass the time, they played games, the boys pinching the girls' asses and the girls' asses biting the boys' asses. Then they tethered all the asses at the church door. One day during the revolution, a bomb fell in the graveyard. In the confusion, everyone jumped through the windows, the boys falling on the girls' asses, the girls on the boys' asses. As to the vicar, he missed his ass altogether and fell in the bomb hole. Which goes to show. . ." Witchbourne paused dramatically. Tarrou and Turbida seemed frozen, their features pale with insulted sensibility. Only Coote, who was hearing the story for the first time, gave the necessary prompt.

"What?" he asked.

"That the Vicar did not know his ass from a hole in the ground," said Mitchell Witchbourne with satisfaction. As the waves of unease spread around the table, he gathered up the cards and rose to his feet. "Beddy bye," he said softly, disappearing off into the darkness. The others looked at each other with the expression of people who did not know what to think, and did not dare ask.

It was in this atmosphere—a harmony woven of night sounds: the warm darkness beyond the veranda, the tinkle of ice-cubes, the rise and fall of voices—that Bernard Corunna Coote felt impelled to his first confession. Having drunk more than usual one night, he announced, with sudden confidential exactness:

"I am a renegade Protestant!"

There was silence for a moment. Then Witchbourne, who was dealing, flicked an eyebrow upwards. "Ach so," he said, in guttural parody.

"We have few Protestants in Central America, as a such," said Turbida. "They do not seem to go with the climate."

"You do not understand," said Coote, beating the table with his glass. "I am a renegade Ulster Protestant."

"I have heard of the Huguenots," said Tarrou politely. "And, of course, the Hussites and Lutherans. But I do not know of your sect: is it interesting, perhaps, like the Catharists or Boggomils—Eros rather than Agape?"

"You still do not understand," said Coote fiercely. "I am a renegade Ulster Presbyterian; an Orangeman!"

"Ah, a regional form of Calvinism," said Tarrou sweetly. "We have had that too: the Jansenists of Port-Royal. But you should not let it worry you." He studied his cards carefully before raising three fingers. "Catholics, Protestants, Communists, *nous sommes tous des assassins.*"

A silence fell, heavy as the night outside. It was broken by the sound of Bernard Corunna Coote weeping: one tear fell, with a distinct plop, into his whiskey glass. His large head, flabby with drink, runnelled with tears, looked like a flayed vegetable marrow. The game continued.

After this rash beginning, Bernard Corunna Coote learned to offer his confidences with the same casualness as he played his cards. And though (unlike the latter) they lay without immediate comment, he knew that they were being picked up, one by one, gestures towards a portrait. Assembled, they made what Tarrou once smilingly called

## LE PETIT TESTAMENT DE BERNARD CORUNNA COOTE.

Bernard Corunna Coote came from a distinguished Ulster family, descendants of Captain William Coote, who was rewarded for his skillful butchery in the Cromwellian campaign with a large grant of Papish land. Industrious in peace as war, he was the founder and first Provost of Strulebridge: an equestrian statue (brave, beetle-browed, a minor hammer of the Lord) still stands in the town square, on the site of an old palace of the O'Neills.

The family seat, however, was at Castlecoote, overlooking the river. At first, little more than a four-square grey farmhouse or "Bawn" (fortified to prevent the sorties of dispossessed Catholic neighbors), it was redesigned by John Nash in 1755. As they watched the new building rise—the doorways flanked with fluted Doric columns, the noble rooms with elliptical designs on the ceilings, the terraces diminishing to the river—something seemed to happen to the family features. ("You could see it in the portraits," said Bernard Corunna Coote, "they felt easier, less predatory, more secure.")

In this handsome Georgian building, generations of Cootes grew up, the eldest managing the estate (and generally the county as well, being Grand Master of the Orange Lodge), the younger going into colonial service, the daughters marrying other Plantation squires, their equals in land and religion. The only break in this pattern came when war broke out: then, as one man, they rushed to the side of the King. Hardheaded, with the bravery of the Irish, but more sense, they made magnificent soldiers, especially when commanding a regiment of their own tenants. A Coote had led the crucial charge at Corunna, a Coote had been aide-de-camp to Wellington, a Coote had led the Ulster division on the Somme. Whenever the Empire was in danger, a Coote would take command, looking at the battlefield as though it were a few hundred acres of his own land and say, with a brisk return to the vernacular: "WULL DRIVE THEM THRU THERE!"

To this tradition, compounded of the sword and the ploughshare, was born a son, Bernard Corunna Coote, a sore disappointment. His whole career seemed a demonstration of the principle of cultural reversion, i.e., the invasion of the conqueror by the culture of the conquered. His childhood was spent listening to old Ma Finnegan, the Catholic tenant in the lodge gate: she taught him the Rosary in Irish and the tests for entering the Fianna. His holidays from public school were spent roaming the hills in a kilt, with an Irish wolfhound at his heels. From these walks sprang his vocation: in his third year at Oxford he announced that he was going to be an archaeologist, an expert on the horned cairns of the Carlingford culture, the burial places of the chieftains of Uladh.

He was on a field trip, deciphering standing stones in the highlands of Donegal, when war broke out in September 1939. Bernard Corunna Coote could no longer resist family tradition: he joined as a volunteer in the North Irish Horse and fought in both the African and Sicilian campaigns. But though he acquitted himself well (whatever else, he was no coward) the contrast between how he regarded himself and what was happening to him became too much to bear. The first his parents heard of it was when he was reported as refusing a decoration "on the grounds that he did not recognize the present King of England." A campaign for the use of Gaelic in Irish regiments also brought comment, coinciding as it did with the preparations for D-Day. Invalided out of the army in 1944, he did not (at his father's request) return to Castlecoote. After rattling about Dublin for a few years, he disappeared to America.

### III

From these confidences, delivered so haltingly, heard so calmly, Bernard Corunna Coote received the peculiar form of comfort which was the secret of the Hotel Darien. His companions spoke rarely of what he had said (the only direct comment was Tarrou's puzzled remark that he did not see what all this had to do with religion), but he knew that it had been heard, and if not understood, accepted. He became one of the members of an invisible club, an enclosed order whose purpose was not so much contemplative as protective: behind these walls they seemed to say, you are safe, all things are equal, you may live as you like. He no longer sought Hautmoc (Lord High Muck, Witchbourne scornfully called him, his name being that of the last Aztec chieftain who tried to propitiate Cortez by a mass sacrifice) for long conferences, though the latter still watched him from behind the pillars of the arcade as he went to collect his letters. Apart from that morning stroll he had been assimilated into the world of the hotel.

It was some months, however, before he was introduced to the second ritual of the permanent residents: the visit to the town whorehouse. Every Sunday afternoon, led by Mitchell Witchbourne, dazzlingly spruce in white ducks and embroidered shirt, they made their way to an old colonial house on the other end of the town. This spacious building belonged to Dona Anna, a mestizo matron whom Witchbourne—remembering some comic strip of his youth about an orphan girl—had nicknamed Obsidian Annie. She was not really an orphan, but the widow of an officer who had taken the wrong side in the Revolution. Finding herself stranded in San Antonio, she had applied her strong, practical nature to developing the primitive prostitution system of the area—the famous ''double-baths'' of festival days—into a regular business. Under her care she had usually about half a dozen young ladies, ranging from sixteen to thirty, with the dusky, almost negroid beauty of the women of the peninsula.

Events at the Casa Anna always followed a definite order, the decorum of Sunday blending with the lady's desire to do her best for her most monied visitors. First, the girls appeared, wearing their holiday best, long flounced skirts, embroidered lace *huipls* or bodices, and heavy earrings made out of United States gold pieces. Dona Anna, of course, being one of *los correctos,* the people of good standing, wore a stiff dress of dark Spanish silk, to distinguish herself from such peasant finery. They all had a social drink together while the men made their choice (there was usually a new recruit to spice routine). Then they withdrew to their rooms where, beside each *palias* stood the inevitable bottle of *tequila*. Through the long afternoon everyone loved or drank or watched through the windows the boys shinning the banana trees, like insects on a grass blade. Now and again there was a satisfying plop! as one fell into the undergrowth.

It seemed a good life.

As darkness gathered, everyone came together again for the evening meal. This took place in the dining hall, the largest room in the house, with fortress-like doors opening onto the patio. At the head of the table presided Obsidian Annie, a clapper by her side to summon the two white-coated Indian house boys. As the food piled higher (local delicacies like turtle eggs, or iguana roe, with purple yams and papayas), a kind of wild gaiety seized them, the girls shrieking as the men pinched them through their thin finery. Even Obsidian Annie relaxed her vigilant decorum, growing nostalgic as she drank from the stone jar of fresh *pulque* at her side. Tears trickled down her thick make-up as she remembered the days when she had been a young girl, the great days before the Revolution: Obsidian Annie was not a democrat.

"And on Sunday we all rode together in Chapultepec Park. Oh, you should have seen us, the girls sitting side-saddle, wearing black hats and skirts, and lovely Spanish leather boots. And the men, with their silver buttons and braids, in the *charro* style, as handsome as Cortez!"

It seemed a more than good life.

The delay in introducing Bernard Corunna Coote to the second ritual of the Hotel Darien was cautionary: they feared that the same forces which had pushed him to total confession would push him further, and that they would lose a hard-won recruit. But they need not have worried; he and Dona Anna got on together like a house on fire. Previously it had been Tarrou who had been her favorite, as coming closest to her aristocratic ideal; in moments of tenderness she called him Maximilian, remembering the blond prince who had tried to bring French civilization to her country.

But between a suave member of the middle-class and something approaching the real thing, there was no question. In clasping Bernard Corunna Coote to her firmly corseted bosom, she clasped her own youth, a bloated version of the *caballeros* who had escorted her through Chapultepec Park. And from her flatteringly warm embrace (a blend of fustian and volcano), he seemed to extract a maternal solace.

True, he had bouts of restlessness, but they were the "thick head" of the novice, rather than real rebellion. Whenever he sulked, refusing to come to the banquets by which she set such store, she went to fetch him. Soon they were drinking and singing together, he calling her "His favorite g-e-l" and teaching her the songs of the Continental Irish brigade:

> On Ramillies field we were forced to yield
> Before the clash of Clare's Dragoons...

The only person upset by this arrangement was Tarrou, who discovered in himself vestiges of a jealousy he thought extinct. But having given up life *as a such* (to use Turbida's phrase), why quarrel with one aspect of it? His wit grew more strained, his stories more silkily sadistic, but his ill-humor did not seem to threaten the equilibrium of their communal life. Not, at least, until the night of the May Festival, several months later.

For the members of the Hotel Darien, the May Festival was the major trial of the year, the one day when the town broke in on their consciousness with an usurping rattle and roar. A famous local patriot had said that a Revolution should be as gay as a Carnival: in his memory, San Antonio made its carnivals as violent as revolutions. From the tolling of the cathedral bell in the morning, through the Blessing of the Goats at midday, to the processions in the evening and the Grand Ball at night, it was one long orgy of noise. Indians in gaudy finery pressed through the street, shouting and waving banners: by nightfall most of them were roaring drunk, challenging all comers with their machetes.

In previous years the inhabitants of the hotel had made half-hearted attempts to join in the fun. But they could never relax or feel at home, the locals parting before them as they came to the wooden beer canteens in the square, their connoisseur's interest in the blind flute-player turned to mockery as they passed, the local matrons parting with relief from their embrace in the dance tent, with its flaring gasoline lamps. As they left, they heard the music spring up again, its vitality underlining their isolation:

> Woman is an apple
> Ripe upon a tree—
> He who least expects it
> May have her beauty free;
> And I pray to San Antonio
> *That it may be me!*

Their object became to close it out of their consciousness. They could not go to Dona Anna's establishment because (cupidity getting the better of her aristocratic inclinations), it was full of drunken Indians. Neither could they relax in the garden or on the terrace: the noise was too great. So they remained indoors, with all the windows and doors locked. But the heat became so intense that they felt they were drowning. Even under the fans there was no relief, the metal wings only stirring the thick air.

By nightfall they had gathered in the hotel lounge, in the vague hope of playing their customary game. But they were all drunk, with that peculiar restlessness, that draining of energy which a day's drinking brings. Together with a nervous irritation: Tarrou's voice was razor-sharp with menace.

"Shall we begin now?" he asked, for the third time.

No one spoke. There was a burst of cheering that made the windows rattle. A firework rose in the air, broke and fell, illuminating the room with a sudden glow.

"Shall we begin?" said Tarrou again, rapping the deck of cards on the table.

Still no one spoke. Another firework climbed within the square of the window. Coote watched it moodily: he felt isolated from the others and had the impression he was missing something.

"I see you are impressed by our peasant customs," said Tarrou, with acidity.

"They do make a lot of noise," Witchbourne interposed.

"You are not the only one, of course," continued Tarrou. "Dona Anna also likes them, although she pretends not to. It is easier to impress peasants."

"But not so much noise as some city people do," said Turbida, hastily joining Witchbourne's rescue operations. "There is a rough night-club behind the Reforma where as soon as the girls appear everyone shouts—" He expired in giggling lecherousness.

But Tarrou was not to be cheated of his prey so easily.

"The noisiest night-club I ever knew was on the borders of the Goutte d'Or district in Paris: you know, the Arab quarter. There was a fat Algerian tout there, a sort of barker. Now that I come to think of it, he resembled our friend here..." He gestured towards Coote, who shifted slightly in his chair. Like an animal entering a slaughterhouse, sensing the glint of steel hooks, he was becoming aware of the menace directed towards him.

"The only time there was silence in that club was during the act involving the Siamese twins. Some day I must tell you about that."

"Some day," said Witchbourne, gruffly.

"I remember—" said Turbida again.

"But the Siamese twins, though an interesting act, lacked the simplicity, the imaginative daring of the barker's own specialty. I have told you he was an Arab. He wore a long flowing burnous: at first I thought it was for local color. But at the end of the evening, he removed it, slowly. It was only then that one realized— *on le soupçonne toujours d'ailleurs, avec les types gros comme ça...*"

"What?" asked Turbida, in spite of himself.

"That he was a woman. A big, fat, ugly, aged woman."

There was silence. Mitchell Witchbourne's face was white. But it was Coote who spoke, finally, dragging his great bulk up.

"You go too far," he said raspingly. "Even in hell there are limits."

## IV

Happiness is a balance, precariously maintained: to achieve even its semblance requires training. While the others, with instincts geared to survival, swept the incident aside, Bernard Corunna Coote clearly could not. For days he avoided the hotel and news drifted back that he and been seen drinking with Hautmoc. After a while, he began coming again to meals, but when Witchbourne ostentatiously produced the card table he disappeared, and they heard him crunching down the avenue towards the town. He did not even return to the Casa Anna, though Obsidian Annie inquired after him, saying that she had seen him (again with Hautmoc) at the local café. It was agreed that Tarrou should speak to him. One night, as Coote was ploughing back through the darkness, the slim Frenchman presented himself at the door, his cold eyes taking— but not returning—the latter's surprised glare.

"We do not see you now," he said pleasantly.

Coote did not answer, all his efforts absorbed in the task of breathing. But he moved forward as though to brush past Tarrou.

"Why do you not join us in the evenings any more?"

Coote stopped. "You know why."

"*Mais, mon ami,*" Tarrou spread his hands, gently. "These things are unimportant. *Dans l'ivresse, comme dans l'amour, il faut tout pardonner.*"

Coote looked at him for a long time, and his eyes seemed to clear in the hallway light. Then he moved forward again, resolutely.

"May mwah, jenny pooh pah," he said, in his harsh Ulster accent.

For his former companions of the Hotel Darien, however, no answer was final. They did not begin to despair of him even when he disappeared on his first "expedition." It looked so harmless, a large man with a morning-after face and stubble, going off into the jungle by himself, carrying a hammer. And the bag of samples he brought back, examining them for hours on the terrace, were like colored beads a child might play with. But when instruments and books began to arrive at the post office and the day's wanderings spread into weeks, they began to be alarmed: in the organized quality of these frenzies, they recognized an alien discipline. Swallowing his pride, Witchbourne went out of his way to speak to Hautmoc, and inquired as to their purpose. The latter graciously accepted the drink offered him, but was far from helpful.

"He is looking for something we have both lost," he said mysteriously.

*Revolver in one hand, machete in the other, his T-shirt moist with sweat (except where the great raft of the sun hat kept a circle of white about his shoulders) he beat his way through the jungle around San Antonio. Behind him followed a retinue of peons, tangle-haired, liquid-eyed, carrying the inevitable burden of impedimenta. With their slow pace, their resigned gestures, they seemed less like human beings than like a column of ants, winding its way patiently over and around obstacles.*

Even the rainy season did not halt him, physical obstacles being only a drum-call to the military ardours of his ancestry. Coming to a flood-swollen river he would plunge in, his weapons held high above his head: sometimes only the hand and the round circle of the hat could be seen as he sidestroked heavily across. If there was a current he would float with it, until he struck an outcrop. Then, like Excalibur, he broke to the surface and trampled ashore, water dripping from his bulk, as though down the side of a mountain. By the time his followers had crossed (going to a village for the loan of a pirogue, or wading downstream until they found a fording place) he had already blazed a trail into the pelvic rankness of the jungle on the other side.

What the Indians thought of their master—a comic *gringo* if ever there was one—was at first tactfully submerged in the fact that he paid well. Sufficiently well for them to want to humor him when, following some atavistic memory of a Victorian jungle trek, he insisted that they should carry their own packs and leave their burros behind. But as the months passed, something of his anxiety communicated to them: just as they sped with eagerness on his errands, so they watched with increasing concern his disappointment as he turned over the stones they had brought.

A man, they knew from their own lives, could only bear so much misfortune: in Bernard Corunna Coote's case they felt that some incongruous struggle was going on, an almost physical rending, as though a blind man were trying to see, or a cripple to walk.

Sometimes he would stop short in his tracks, as if struck by a blow from behind. The pale blue eyes would glaze and turn inwards, the shoulders hunch, until he looked like the oldest of earth's creatures, some grey mammoth embedded in ice or rock. And the cry that he gave, low at first, rose till it seemed beyond human pitch, a trumpeting that tore the heart with its animal abandon.

It was after one of these outbreaks (dutifully reported by the servants), that the inhabitants of the Hotel Darien decided that a last effort should be made to save Bernard Corunna Coote for themselves. For to their surprise they had discovered that they needed him. From selfish exasperation at the loss of a necessary companion, they had passed to real concern, and an emotion that only their long habits of reticence refused to recognize as love. It was as though their bluff had been called, and the suffering they had gradually relegated to the background of their own lives had suddenly reappeared before them, monstrous, dishevelled, wringing its hands.

But what was to be done? They had a formal meeting in the hotel lounge ("the scene of the crime" as Turbida said brightly, before Tarrou's coldly speculative eye fell upon him) to discuss the situation. Tarrou's attempt to apologize had failed. Witchbourne's efforts to elicit information from Hautmoc had been fruitless. There remained Turbida, the soiled innocent of the party, whom no one would ever suspect of any serious motive. Witchbourne's mild eye joined Tarrou's in resting upon him. Turbida must find out what Bernard Corunna Coote thought he was doing.

The opportunity came a few days later when Coote returned from a long absence in the jungle. He looked more exhausted than ever, with a rough growth of beard and a tear in his trousers which exposed long thin legs. But he did not seem surprised to find Turbida in his room, his expensive shape splayed over a cane chair.

"Good day—?" the latter asked, with the upward inflection of the hunting classes.

Bernard Corunna Coote snorted, but did not answer. After depositing a sack in a corner, he dragged off his clothes, and stepped under the shower. Through the yellow curtain Turbida could see his body, a whale under water.

"I have been looking at your books," shouted Turbida, lifting up a volume with a large painting of a pyramid on the cover.

Still no answer. The shower sank, a hand groped for a towel: Bernard Corunna Coote emerged, clean spiky haired, decently clothed in white.

"Interesting chaps, these Aztecs, when you get right down to it," continued Turbida, turning the pages. "Place like Monte Alban now, makes you think..."

Coote stopped pummelling himself. "You have been to Monte Alban?" he asked incredulously.

"Why, yes," said Turbida, trying desperately to remember the illustration Tarrou had shown him, "and to Mitla too."

"Did you see the scrollwork at Mitla? The cruciform chambers?"

"Yes, yes..." encored Turbida.

"The spiral and lozenge pattern are the same as at Newgrange. It was a characteristic of the race, the delight in abstract pattern. But we were a thousand years before."

Turbida was about to inquire where Newgrange was when he saw that Coote was no longer listening to him, his face contorted with fury and anguish.

"Think of it! When Cortez and his Spaniards came, they found the Maltese cross, and the Indians spoke of strange white men. Certainly it was Brendan—"

"Brendan?" echoed Turbida.

"Saint Brendan who discovered America. But what about even earlier? We know that the Celts were a widely dispersed people: traces of them have been found in Sardinia, Galicia, the valley of the Dordogne. We are the secret mother race of Europe. But if—" he halted, as though transfixed by the daring of his thought.

"If," prompted Turbida.

"We could prove that the Celts not merely discovered but *founded* America! Think of it—" He brought his face close to that of Turbida, who could smell the furnace blast of cheap spirits.

"Then, for the first time, the two halves of the world would fit together, into one, great, universal Celtic civilization." He raised his arms high, then let them fall slowly again. "All I need is a proof."

"Like what?" asked Turbida in a hushed voice.

"Oh, there are minor ones. Character for example; Hautmoc

says that the original Indians were the purest race in the western hemisphere: we still place a great emphasis on purity. And *physique;* remember the bearded statues of La Venta?" He tugged his own beard vehemently, to emphasize each word. "After us, there were no bearded men in South America."

"But a major proof?"

Coote seemed to hesitate. It was months since he had spoken to anyone: should he now reveal his hopes to a comparative stranger? Only the music of international renown could heal several generations of outraged tradition: here, in San Antonio, Bernard Corunna Coote was staging his last fight to restore himself not merely to his family, but to the whole history of human knowledge.

"I told you once of the cairns of Carlingford and the Boyne, the burial places of our early chieftains. From the decorative motifs I deduce a connection between them and the pyramids of the lost civilizations of Central America. But the pyramids, according to Hautmoc, were designed for human sacrifice only, and not for ritual interment. If I could find..."

He hesitated again, drew a deep breath.

"Somewhere, in the most remote areas, probably in the thick of the jungle, there must be traces of those earlier structures upon which Monte Alban, Palenque, Chichén Itzá, were based. If I could find one single passage grave or burial chamber..."

"Like what?" asked Turbida again.

"Like this!" cried Bernard Corunna Coote, seizing and opening a large green volume. "Look!"

Carlos Turbida was still trembling when he joined the others an hour later.

"But the man is mad," he cried plaintively.

"The question is irrelevant," said Witchbourne, with unaccustomed severity. "Which of us is even half sane?" His gaze swept across his companions, like a searchlight across rocky ground.

"Still, it is strange," said Tarrou. "I was sure he was cured. Who would have thought the irrelevant could have such deep roots?"

"But nothing can be done. It is too late..." wailed Turbida again.

"It is never too late," said Witchbourne sententiously. "While there's life there's hope. What do you think, Tarrou?"

"I think," said Tarrou, "that the time has come for our famous reckoning." From his pocket he produced a sheaf of white dockets, neatly bound with rubber: he ruffled it under their noses.

"A sum of money is always useful," agreed Witchbourne.

"But then, what will you do?" asked Turbida.

Tarrou shrugged. "We shall see. I will perhaps go and talk to our noble friend, Lord High Muck."

"But what about?"

"About literature," smiled Tarrou. "Where is that book you say Coote gave you?"

V

The rainy season passed. The mouth of the San Antonio River was no longer choked by floating vegetation, and the long dugout canoes could sail directly up to the market place. The mountain paths had dried and the peasants came down to the village in ox-carts, lined with layers of crushed sugar-cane. The few meager crops were to be harvested, maize, sesame seeds, beans. Soon the first tourist bus would turn into the square, to halt for an hour or so before continuing its journey southward.

It was on the anniversary of their first meeting that Hautmoc came to Bernard Corunna Coote with unexpected news. The latter was sitting at his accustomed place on the terrace: he had not been on trek for over a week, and looked more than usually morose, his shoulders slouched over the café table. Behind him hovered the proprietor, fearful not that he would attack anyone (despite his noise, the gross foreigner was surprisingly gentle, not like the common-class of Indians who broke loose with their machetes when drunk) but that he should do himself harm: the day before he had fallen on his way to the lavatory. Now and again, from that seemingly quiescent mound of flesh, a hand would emerge, and grope around the table for the bottle which was poured, with many whistling sighs and groans, in and around his glass.

It was then that Hautmoc appeared on the far side of the square near the post-office. It was hard to miss him because, after several months of unaccustomed prosperity, he had deserted his trampish practices and dressed as befitted a descendant of kings, with an elegant *serape,* slashed in scarlet and black, and a white sombrero. Moreover he was walking briskly, almost running, with an abandon that surprised Bernard Corunna Coote, who had been talking to him only the night before. He came directly to the café table, but did not sit down, gazing at his friend and employer with a kind of tranced look:

"Master," he said solemnly, "we may have news."

Bernard Corunna Coote stirred. "What do you mean, you may have news?" he grated.

Hautmoc looked over his shoulder, towards the café-owner, indicating that he did not feel free to speak. "We may have important news," he repeated.

With an effort, Coote threw out his arm towards the chair opposite him. "Sit down and have a drink."

"There is no time," said Hautmoc. He leaned his head swiftly down towards the other's sunken face, and whispered into his ear: "We have found what you were looking for."

Bernard Corunna Coote started. Did Hautmoc know what he was saying? Like the shepherd boy suddenly face to face with the wolf, like the alchemist seeing a yellow liquid condense in his crucible, he gazed at him, slowly believing his eyes.

"Where?" he asked, rising from the table.

The sun was low in the sky on their second day's march when they reached the area indicated by Hautmoc. It lay near the source of the San Antonio River, a region Coote had rarely explored, believing it already well known to the natives. But perhaps he had been wrong to ignore it: after all, river-beds were the traditional centers of civilization. But so high up? For hours they had climbed up the mountainside, through the thick forest of the lower slopes, where springs made the ground soggy and treacherous. Then they crossed a belt of shale and rock, where the river sank to a trickle, and they found animal skeletons bleaching in the sun. Finally, towards evening, they emerged onto a small plateau set, like a shelf, against the steep incline.

A light wind was blowing. Below them, the valley fell away, a matted sea of vegetation, divided by the thin line of the river. There was no sign of a living thing, the smoke from the occasional village or clearing being absorbed in the transparent mist that lay above the trees. At the limit of their view the sun was sinking, like a coal at the heart of a dying fire.

"Is this the place?" said Bernard Corunna Coote, impatiently.

After easing off their packs, the Indians had gathered around him and Hautmoc, as though waiting for an order. The latter did not answer, but remained looking out, in melodramatic serenity.

"Is this the place?" asked Coote again. "Where is it, or what is it called?"

"It is called Coatlicue," said Hautmoc seriously. "It is one of the most ancient of our sacrificial grounds. The people took refuge here during the Conquest. There used to be a temple."

"But where—" demanded Coote.

"Behind," said Hautmoc. Folding his *serape* around him, an elegant figure in scarlet and black, he turned to lead the way.

In his excitement at the view, Bernard Corunna Coote had not yet had time to look behind him. Now, following Hautmoc, he turned. Above them rose a rock face, sheer as a wall, making the area in which they stood seem artificially compact, like an apron stage. The outer edge of the plateau was covered with a hide of tough yellow grass, knotted so close that it made walking difficult. This yielded to a close undergrowth, where lichened boulders lay around like ruins: to Coote's astonishment there was the semblance of a path through it, stained with burro droppings. This led to a clump of well-watered trees: was it the source of the river? Parting the damp oar-shaped leaves, Bernard Corunna Coote saw an open space ahead, a clearing at the entrance of which Hautmoc and his fellow Indians had gathered to await him.

In the middle of the clearing stood a group of stones. As he drew closer—scattering the natives to right and left like ninepins—he saw that they formed a shape, the unmistakable humped outline of a tumulus. There were two stones on either side, with a closed passage at the far end. There was the great flagstone, resting on the five stones as smoothly as a table top. The whole thing was symmetrical, textbook perfect, even the dark quiet faces grouped around seemed in harmony—except for one thing. As Coote approached, his foot crushed something in the grass. Whoever had hoisted the flagstone had forgotten to remove the pulley rope. It wound imperceptibly down the crevice between the two nearest side stones until, like a snake, its end struck up at the sole of Coote's sandal.

He stood there, looking from the rope to the construction, and back again. Then he followed the rope to its source, under the top stone, and tugged. The stone shifted, audibly. He stepped back and gazed for a long time, until even the Indians—professionals of the steady gaze—felt uneasy. Their leader came over and touched him on the shoulder but Coote did not move.

"Master," said Hautmoc gently, "we meant no harm."

Coote still did not reply, his eye rolling over the same square of space, like an eager student crazed for an answer.

"We would not have known how to build it, but for Señor Tarrou. He taught us. And Señors Witchbourne and Turbida provided the money for the workers."

Coote looked at him. "But you, why did you do it? You told me you would have nothing to do with them."

The dark face of the Indian seemed to crease and open, as though reliving a painful decision.

"They"—he pointed to his fellows around—"did it because they wished to please you. I—" he hesitated.

"Yes?" demanded Coote.

"I did it because—because if the place you are searching for does not exist, then it should. Your dream and mine have much in common."

Coote looked at his companion for a long time. Then a hint of a smile crossed his face.

"Hautmoc," he said, with majesty, "you are even madder than I am."

But the other was not listening, his eyes resting fondly on the stones before him. "There is still one thing lacking to prove us both right," he said sadly. "Such stones cry out to be used."

For a long time Coote's expression did not change, as if he had not understood what Hautmoc had said. Then he straightened, his great back cracking, and looked at the Indians around. They returned his gaze with expectant, admiring eyes, as though his countenance reflected the pure bronze light of the dying solar god. Knowledge passed swiftly across his face, a spasm of lightning.

"I understand," he said gravely.

Slowly, with the dignity of a military ceremony, he removed his large sun hat. His face was a hunk of meat, fiery red, but above it his bald head shone, the whitest thing they had ever seen. He stepped briskly forward, the Indians falling in line behind him. When he came to the passage grave he marched straight in, leaving them to file to one side, where the loose rope dangled.

"Pull," he ordered, settling himself in the trough of red clay. As he waited for the heavens to fall, his countenance became relaxed and pure, all provincial crudity refined to a patrician elegance, the ripe intensity of a soldier leader born of two great traditions. Softly on fields of history, Ramillies and El Alamein, Cremona and the Somme, the warpipes began to grieve. Closing ranks, ghostly regiments listened, Connaught Rangers and Clare's Dragoons, Dublin and Inniskilling Fusiliers, Munsters and Royal Irish, North Irish Horse and Sarsfield's Brigade. The stone started to creak.

"After all, it is a good way for a chieftain to die," he thought contentedly.

from *Death of a Chieftain*

## COATLICUE

In the title story of *Death of a Chieftain,* I referred to Coatlicue as the Aztec God of Death. She is, of course, feminine, "the Goddess with the skirt of snakes," and she quickly had her revenge for my tactlessness.

Your body is small,
squat, deformed as
a Nahautl Indian,
an Aztec image
of necessary death:

casually born
of the swirl of
a river, tossed
up by tides—
sexual flotsam—

regard those swart
small breasts that
will never give milk
though around inflamed
nipples, love-bites

multiply like stars.
Salt wind of desire
upon the flesh!
Black hair swings
over your shoulders

as you bear darkness
down toward me, and
across the sun-robed
pyramid, obsidian knives
resume their sacrifice.


from *A Chosen Light*

## COMPANY
### I.M. Theodore Roethke

There is no hawk among my friends.
Swiftly they cruise their chosen air,
Not to spy the grey fieldmouse
And plummet fiercely to the moor,
But to survey a heaven, inspect
The small, the far. Is it new
That the beetle's back is abstract,
A jewel box; the ash-pod has glider wings?
Cruelty is not their way of life,
Nor indifference; they ride the currents
To grasp the invisible. The service
They do shapes also what they are
And the fernlike talon uncurls:
There is no hawk among my friends.


from *A Chosen Light*

## *BEYOND THE LISS**
### *for Robert Duncan*

Sean the hunchback, sadly
Walking the road at evening
Hears an errant music,
Clear, strange, beautiful,

And thrusts his moon face
Over the wet hedge
To spy a ring of noble
Figures dancing, with—

A rose at the center—
The lustrous princess.

Humbly he pleads to join,
Saying, "pardon my ugliness,
Reward my patience,
Heavenly governess."

Presto! like the frog prince
His hump grows feather
Light, his back splits,
And he steps forth, shining

Into the world of ideal
Movement where (stripped
Of stale selfishness,
Curdled envy) all

Act not as they are
But might wish to be—
Planets assumed in
A sidereal harmony—

Strawfoot Sean
Limber as any

But slowly old habits
Reassert themselves, he
Quarrels with pure gift,
Declares the boredom

Of a perfect music,
And, with toadish nastiness,
Seeks first to insult,
Then rape, the elegant princess.

Presto! with a sound
Like a rusty tearing
He finds himself lifted
Again through the air

To land, sprawling,
Outside the hedge,
His satchel hump securely
Back on his back.

*Sean the hunchback, sadly*
*Walking the road at evening.*


from *A Chosen Light*

---

*liss: a fairy mound or fort

## *A BALLAD FOR BERRYMAN*

John, a letter or a song
to celebrate our heady hours together;
memories to warm this filthy Irish weather,
of that long dreepy Dublin winter
we both had to suffer.

Hot toddies in Beggar's Bush
while you decanted another rush
or run of your fermenting *Dream Songs*.
I was still young, aghast at genius,
concerned about your happiness,

Finding a place, pals for evening,
a practical hero-worshipper, only half understanding
your long turmoil or *hegira*
from our first meeting in Iowa
to Jack Ryan's barn-like bar.

Soon after, you came through Paris,
blundered your way up the Rue Daguerre.
To Esteban, working under his cameo of Baudelaire,
you slowly pronounced in stentorian French:
*"ou est le poète Irlandais?"*

and Claude soft-footed across the way:
*"il y a un Moïse Americain
qui te demande."* Behold, behind him
then your great beard appeared; Henry,
grinning from ear to ear.


from *Mount Eagle*

## SINNSEAR: KINDRED
### for Edward Kennedy

In a dream, I was walking
with your two brothers
through the epic landscape
of the Great Tain;
blue crags of Carlingford
and South Armagh.

They listened silently
as I traced and tracked
the slight but rockstrewn slopes
where another hero had withstood.
Bound to a pillarstone, the raven
circles over his drooping head.

Pale blue of a summer evening
was clear enough to show a man
opening a field under Slieve Gullion
with his small plough and team
as their forebears might have done.

Human destiny did not seem so different;
all mythologies are local,
courage related to time and place.
A far-off cottage window flashed, like Morse,
or the final fall of Cuchulain's shield.

Footsteps of someone approaching
by the sun-warmed gable of the barn
caused Robert to turn,
bending into shadow the still unbroken
column of his neck, as John
already had the back of his still shapely head.

*(1978)*

## VIETNAM

Our founding fathers carried guns.
A thunderjet's evaporating sigh
makes a brief and savage music
across an endless urban sky:

but all the flying wealth of Calvin
could not dislodge one limpet nation
from its ancient tenured rock.

So an older world questions the new
which recoils, ashamed, upon itself.

*(1977)*

## *BLUEGRASS*
### *for Dillon Johnstone*

Flying so far to refind my neighbours:
MacLean the gelder recast as a rancher,
Bluegrass acres reaching a wide sky,
While Sheriff Clarke patrols the streets
With a telescopic rifle, cans of teargas.

"Those goddam shitkickers let us down,
You know what I mean, poor class whites
Breaking up the town on Saturday nights."
Womanless cowboys, finding their release
Across the border, in a Mex whorehouse.

"And now those godamned Spicks are hoping
To outvote us, crossing the river at night,
Sneaking up slowly from town to town;
They whelp like rabbits, not like humans:
We'd need another Alamo, to face 'em down.

You're lucky to be mixed up with poetry,
Something that gives a pretty smell to life.
See my wife and daughter in their gowns?
I'm proud to have sent my women folk,
But I never had no time for no University."

I stray from the bourbon lush party,
To the wood panelled quiet of the library.
Not a book in sight, but inside glass cases,
Flintlock and duelling pistol, a silver Colt;
With the family Bible, the treasures of the house.

*(1971)*

## *PACIFIC LEGEND*

In their houses beneath the sea
the salmon glide, in human form.

They assume their redgold skin
to mount the swollen stream,

Wild in the spawning season;
a shining sacrifice for men!

So throw back these bones again:
they will flex alive, grow flesh

When the ruddy salmon returns,
a lord to his underwater kingdom.


from *Mount Eagle*

## *A SLOW DANCE*

I—BACK

Darkness, cave
drip earth womb

we move slowly
back to our origins

the naked salute
to the sun disc

the obeisance
to the antlered tree

the lonely dance
on the grass


earth darkness
clouded moon

whirling arms
they shuffle

hair flying
eyes flashing

instep echoing
one, two as

bare heels, toe
smite the earth


from *A Slow Dance*

## *THE EVOLVING LOGOS*
### *(at the grave of Tielhard de Chardin)*

A Jesuit graveyard recalls a military cemetery,
small white stones standing to attention,
orderly as that other trim forest of the dead;
the white crosses glooming above the Somme,
trumpeting mutely forth the resurrection.

French aristocrat, bearer of the enclitic "de,"
you now lie between MacQuade and Reilly,
footsoldiers in the army of Jesus,
you who were earth's theologian;
servant of the evolving logos, who sought
in Chinese deserts to decipher
the living book of our universe.

A gaunt calvary broods on a hillock
above you and your fallen comrades;
the three veiled and mourning women,
the shadowy figure of the nailed Christ,
the dead center of your world as priest.

In winter there are tracks to your grave
through the snow. In summer, flowers.
Each evening, the last rays of the sun
serve to strike your tomb, above Goodman's lordly Hudson.

*(1985)*

## *POETRY CLASS*
### *for Judy Johnson*

St. Valentine's day
and the rich red wine
of the South pouring.

But you have a job
to do, a class to lead,
a workshop gathering

So our leisurely con-
sideration of our own
and the wide world's

Problems, the stumbling
of some of our colleagues
into the happy farm, or

Down the brief bubble
at the bottle's mouth;
all our friendly manics,

Their antic dispositions
must wait, as we turn
towards uncreased youth.

Still eager, it appears
to be led down the old
beguiling primrose path

To become poets, that
bewildering medley of
the tender & the tough

Publicly useless but
somehow dangerous in
their addiction to truth.

*(1988)*

## *MAGIC CARPET*

I have been up here for days.
No, let's be exact, I have been
up here for months, for half
a year nearly, dreaming time
has finally stopped, meanness
been put to rout, the world
become safe for lovers, poets

And all the rest of us, as well
as we had ever wanted. No need
to bustaxi trudge to the airport,
just slip on the magic carpet,
from Cork to Upstate New York,
from Altcloghfin to Albany, dream-
ing a haven that is suddenly real.

No need even to uncork the bottle,
with this private source of ambrosia,
up so high, it feels like flying
or dying, a lifting of the mind's wings
with you beside me, of course,
uxorious as the Lee's coupled swans,
those abrupt gleams of the marvellous.

Yes, so high up here, so restful
that all that toil seems meaningful,
and drudgery, seen properly, a cheer
of appreciation gone a shade wrong,
a hiccup of homage to the glorious process.
But is this paradisal, this Dantean
spaceship, yet another form of deception,

This autumnal glow, a dangerous elation?
I tell you straight off, I am in
no hurry to come hurtling, or sailing down
as my little personal plane beats on, all
around me, such a snowcloud of lightness,
like a drift of swan feathers in a bedroom,
that, the dashboard flickering, I start to sing.

*(1988)*

822 RM FS
03/30/98 32550